CHECKMATE
Written by Lindsey Powell

novel, Checkmate, are the property of the songwriters and copyright holders.

Other books by Lindsey Powell

The Perfect Series
Perfect Stranger
Perfect Memories
Perfect Disaster
Perfect Beginnings

Part of Me Series
Part of Me
Part of You
Part of Us

Stand-alone
Take Me
Fixation
Checkmate

Prologue
Joey

Be cruel to be kind. Shit, that's been my life motto for as long as I can remember. Becoming a ruthless bastard in order to protect anyone that meant a goddamn thing to me.

I've survived in this world despite all of the odds being against me.

My name is well-fucking-known in the underworld. It's a blessing and a curse. Not many people bother me, because they know what I am capable of. They know that I follow through with my threats.

But when she walked into my life, she blew everything I ever knew to shit.

Paige fucking Daniels, the woman that invaded my cold-blooded heart and then ripped my fucking soul to shreds.

She is my kryptonite.

She is my only fucking weakness, so she had to go.

I couldn't fully bring her into my world. The guns, the violence, the drugs. To bring her in would have made her a target, and it would have shown everyone my Achilles heel.

She made me laugh.

She made me love.

And she made me break her fucking heart.

I always knew that this world was cruel, but I never realised just what it would cost me in the long run.

Paige.

The woman that sets my soul on fire. The woman that has my heart. And the woman that I have to let go.

Being a leader comes with responsibility and learning to live without the things that we cherish the most.

After my meeting with Raymond, my right-hand man, I realised that I can't rule this world and keep her too. The two things don't go together. I've seen men break from losing their loved ones. I've witnessed it time and time again, and my meeting with Raymond showed me just how much he is haunted by losing his wife, Antonia. She was killed in cold-blood by another family. They wanted to hit Raymond where it hurt, and they fucking succeeded. All I can say is, they better be good at hiding, because we're going to hunt the bastards down and wipe their existence off the face of the earth.

I can't risk the same thing happening to Paige. It would kill me, eat me up and fucking destroy me if she were to be killed because of who I am.

I won't take that risk.

I have to do the right thing.

My father's words come back to haunt me. "If you love someone in this life, son, learn to let them go."

Learn to let them go.

Shit.

Hardest fucking thing I will ever have to do.

With a heavy heart, I call out her name and hear her shout, "In here, big guy."

I walk towards the bedroom, and when she comes into view, I almost lose my resolve to get her away from me. She's on the bed, naked, waiting for me, and I'm about to become the biggest asshole that she has ever met.

I had to push her away in the cruellest way possible. She will never forgive me, but I can live with that as long as she is safe.

Safe from my world, safe from the danger, and safe from me.

My reputation stopped me from having her.

My role in this life stopped me from having her.

Throwing her away like a piece of trash turned me into an even meaner motherfucker than I already was.

Giving up the one good thing in my life left me with a bitter taste for revenge.

I want out, and it won't be easy. She doesn't need to witness any part of what is to come. She doesn't deserve to be tainted by me any more than she already has been.

I have a plan to get the fuck out, even if I die trying.

Paige

You know those moments, the ones that hit you right at your core, and leave you feeling like you are on cloud nine?

The moments that define our lives, and mould us into who we are today.

The moments that leave us breathless, and constantly searching for the next high.

That's how he made me feel.

That's what every second of being with him felt like.

Glorious, mind blowing, all consuming.

Moments that would stay locked in my heart forever, until the day that he ripped those moments apart and shattered my heart.

Lying in bed, naked, waiting for him to come back has got to be one of my favourite ways to kill some time. The way he makes love to me, fucks me and leaves me feeling like a goddamn goddess is like nothing else.

I love him, and he loves me.

He may act like a hard-ass, but I get to see the softer side of him, and I love every single second of it.

I don't need anything else in life other than him.

"Paige," I hear him call out. Speak of the delicious devil and he shall appear.

"In here, big guy," I shout back, waiting for him to appear and fill the doorway with his tall frame, broad shoulders, muscular arms and thick thighs, which he does no more than five seconds later.

God, he really does take my breath away.

His eyes take in the sheet that pools around me, my breasts uncovered, my nipples stood to attention. His gaze slowly moves up, his face giving nothing away, but his words make my heart start to pound, and not in a good way.

"Get dressed," he barks as he bends down and picks my dressing robe up off the floor, throwing it towards me.

"Why? Are we going somewhere?" I ask him.

"I'm not, but you are."

What?

"Excuse me?" I say as move from the bed and put the robe on, wrapping it around my body tightly.

"You need to leave, Paige," he says, causing my whole world to shift.

"Leave? Why?" I ask, wondering what happened in the last hour for him to tell me that I need to go.

"Because I said so."

"Because you said so?" I repeat his words sarcastically. "And you think that I am leaving here without a reason for this sudden turn-around?"

Jesus, yesterday he told me I was his fucking everything, and now he's saying I need to leave?

"Yes, Paige, because I fucking said so." His voice echoes around the room, his words turning my world upside down.

"But, why? What did I do?" I sound pathetic even to my own ears, but this man is my life. I can't be without him.

"You didn't do anything."

"Then what the fuck happened? You left me here an hour ago and everything was fine, but now... Now you're making me feel like I'm an inconvenience."

"Maybe you are," he says and the first piece of my heart breaks.

"You don't mean that," I whisper, shaking my head from side to side.

He scoffs. "Don't I? And what makes you the fucking expert on what I mean and what I don't?"

I take a deep breath, trying to calm the rage boiling inside of me.

"Because I know you. You don't want me to leave, so what's really going on here?" I ask, hands on hips, trying to hold my own.

"You have been nothing but a distraction when I've needed it," he says, his face hard.

"A distraction? That's bullshit," I say, struggling to understand why he is being like this.

"It's not bullshit, Paige, and we're done."

He goes to turn away from me and I panic. I surge forwards, moving around him so I am standing in front of him, stopping him from walking away from me.

"Don't do this, don't ruin us and what we have," I say as I rest my hands on his chest. He looks down, his eyes trained on my fingers as I grasp his shirt. "You love me, I know that you love me... Please don't shut me out," I plead, practically begging him not to cast me aside.

He takes a breath, I hold mine.

His ice blues connect with my stormy greys. Except, they probably don't look stormy right now, more like sad and desperately hoping that he isn't going to follow through with this.

His lips part, his shoulders tense, and I can already see that he's closing down, putting his walls into place.

"We've had fun, we've messed around, but I no longer have a place for you in my life." His words cut deep, like a knife straight to my heart.

"No," I whisper as the first tear falls down my cheek.

"Yes. I don't need a distraction anymore, Paige. You were a good fuck, but that's all it ever was for me, a fuck and nothing more."

"You're lying," I manage to say as the tears fall faster.

He shrugs his shoulders. "Believe what you want but make no mistake that we are done here."

I grasp his shirt harder, not wanting to let go. If I let go, I know that I won't get him back, and I won't survive losing him. I'll never get over the heartbreak.

"Please... Please don't do this," I say as I sob. "I love you, I love you so much."

"Well, you're going to have to learn to live without loving me. Take it and give it to someone who deserves it. I'm not the person for you, Paige, and the longer you drag this out, the harder it will be," he says, his voice stern, never wavering.

"Harder for who?"

His jaw tenses and he steps back until I'm no longer fisting my fingers in his shirt. My arms fall to my sides, and I know that I have lost him. The love of my life. The only man to ever make me feel.

"You need to get dressed, pack your stuff up and go, now," he barks, ignoring my previous question.

"You're going to regret doing this."

"I don't regret anything," he says, and the piece of my heart that broke first has the rest of the pieces scattered around it.

"Tell me that you don't love me, and that you never have, and I'll go," I say, forcing him to voice the words that may shatter me beyond repair. If he never loved me, then I need to hear it.

He takes a step forward and bends down a little, so that we are eye-level.

"I don't love you, and I never did."

The air whooshes out of me.

My legs struggle to keep me upright.

And I realise that whatever the game was here, I just fucking lost.

Love is fragile, like glass. If you don't handle it with care, it will fall and break, leaving tiny little fragments in its wake that you will be finding days later.

In my case, the days turned into weeks, and the weeks turned into months.

There is no end in sight for my pain.

There is no happy ending for me.

It's over.

Prince Charming doesn't exist.

True love doesn't exist.

I am living proof. Broken beyond repair and struggling to move past all that I knew.

Joey Valentine did that to me.

He crushed my soul. Trampled on it and made sure that it was ripped apart.

You see, the problem with love is that it makes you blind.

Blind to faults.

Blind to the truth, and blind to the person that you love the most in the world hurting you, like you were nothing but a fucking pawn in the game.

I was his pawn.

He played me and won.

And he's still living the high life whilst I'm roaming in the gutter.

I was just a game to him, someone to relieve him of his stress as he worked his way up to where he is today, and then he threw me away like trash.

He may have played and won, but he isn't expecting my revenge.

He won't see it coming, and I'll be the one to call checkmate.

Chapter One
Paige
Three years later

I exit the car and stare at the building in front of me. The sheer size of the hotel overwhelming me. Large bay windows, flowers lining each one, red bricks, and a huge set of wooden doors make this a place for the rich and famous. Because that's who will be here tonight. The rich for sure, the famous being a little different than the A-list stars of this world.

The famous people here tonight are all criminals. Well known, respected, and likely to shoot a motherfucker's head off for so much as looking at them in the wrong way. Dangerous, yes. Exciting, maybe. Intimidating, not so much.

You see, I've had dealings with all of these criminal assholes for the last two years. I worked my way up from gutter rat to boss bitch. I did it for me, and because it was all I knew at the time.

Leaving school with no qualifications and having Joey Valentine throw me away like trash meant that I was at a loss as to what to do with my life. He always thought that he hid his criminal world dealings from me so well, but little did he know that I was taking it all in from the side lines. I watched, I kept quiet, and I retained any piece of information I overheard. Joey tried to keep me away from his business, but I would sneak around, listening in, just so that I could feel closer to him. I was desperate; I needed him like I needed air to breathe.

And now? Now I need no one. He taught me not to trust easily, and boy has that come in handy over the years. Joey shattering my heart to pieces was the best thing that ever happened to me. It made me who I am today. Strong, independent, and fucking respected.

It's not often that women get the respect that they deserve in the underworld, but I did. I'm only twenty-nine but I made it, and Joey Valentine is going to look like he's shitting broken glass when I am done with him.

I thank my driver and smooth down the front of my gown. Black lace that hangs down to the floor, slits either side of the skirt that go to the tops of my thighs, and thin straps over my shoulders, the corseted top hugging my womanly curves. My blond hair is hanging down loose and poker straight. The accompanying eye makeup is dark like my soul, the deep red of my lipstick standing out against my fair skin. And the black stilettos with the red heels, fucking stunning, if I do say so myself. I am a sucker for a beautiful shoe, and these are no exception.

I carry a small black clutch purse with me, containing my handgun. There is no need for anything else. I won't have to pay for a thing this evening, and my boys are on standby at my house, meaning I don't have to carry keys with me. I exude the bitch boss vibe, and tonight I will get to show every asshole in that room who I am. They all know me by the name of Miss Roderick. Not Miss Daniels. I dropped that name when Joey dropped me and kept my first name a secret. Never let them in. Never allow them close.

I keep my cards close to my chest, never meeting with the assholes that I am about to reveal myself to. It gives me power, and I know that every man in that room tonight will fucking hate the fact that I have controlled my empire whilst remaining in the shadows.

I conduct my business through my right hand man, Donovan. But tonight that will all change. And there is only one person in that room that knows my first name is Paige,

and he will wish that he had never laid eyes on me,
because once I am done with him, he is going to be the
one with the shattered heart.

Chapter Two
Joey

God, this kind of shit bores the ass off of me. I've been doing events like this for as long as I can remember, and I have never once enjoyed them. The people in this room all think that they are worth something, and that others should bow down to them. Well, everyone except me, because I bow to no one. I run the motherfucking game, and they all know it.

There are some of the most revolting, underhanded assholes in this room, but none of them have ever taken me on. They know better. The purpose of this evening is to show them all who the top dog is, and never let them forget.

However, there will be one face here tonight that intrigues me ever so slightly. Miss Roderick, the woman who is throwing this party. A woman that I am yet to meet, but one that has been making waves in the underhand business that we all have dealings in. She seems to have come from nowhere, and I wonder how the fuck she has managed it. I've run these streets for the last five years, and it wasn't until a couple of months ago that I heard her name mentioned.

I requested a meeting with her, but that was shot down. No one here knows what she looks like, and her reputation is up there with the best of them. I want to know how she rose to fame without so much as a hint to who the fuck she is.

I have gathered enough intel in here tonight to know that she runs rings around some of the major players. She seems to have a hold on each of them, getting them to do whatever the fuck she wants, and she does all this as a faceless woman.

I cannot comprehend how, but I'm going to have that question answered tonight. I can feel the ripple of excitement in the room at her impending arrival. Most of the men in here just want a glimpse of her, to see if they will able to get in her fucking pants and claim the woman that holds so much power. The others will just be waiting to size up their competition, me included. If this woman thinks that she is about to walk in here and take the top spot, then she is sadly fucking mistaken.

No one takes anything from me. Not ever. Period.

"Mr Valentine," a waitress purrs at the side of me as she holds a tray filled with glasses of champagne.

I look at her with distaste. I have no interest in women that have their tits pushed up to their neck and their make-up on so thick that you would wake up next to a fucking stranger in the morning. No woman has ever come close to Paige. And I wouldn't want them to.

I shake my head as an image of Paige forms in my mind. I don't like to think about her. I know that I ruined her, and if I let myself think about that, then the rage that I have held inside of me all of these years would come out, and not even I want to think about what the result would be.

"Champagne, sir?" the waitress asks, her tone pissing me off with how sickly sweet it is.

"I'm good," I reply. No please, no thank you.

Her face falls and she nods her head at me before scurrying away and finding the next asshole to try and hit on.

Women think this world is glamorous and glitzy. Fancy cars, designer clothes, diamonds around their necks, wrists or placed on their fingers. But they don't see the shit that goes down on a daily basis. They have no idea what it takes to get your name to the top and for people to bow the fuck down to you. At least most women don't. But the one that is about to make her entrance into this room clearly knows the deal. She clearly understands what this world entails, and she has used it to her advantage.

The doors open, and the crowd comes to a standstill. All eyes look towards the door. Not a sound to be heard over the clicking of her heels as she enters the room. Her head is bowed, a long, black lace dress with thigh high slits at each side adorns her body, fuck-me black shoes on her feet. I allow my eyes to roam up her body slowly.

I may not be interested in having a woman on my arm, but even I can appreciate the fact that her body is killer. Perfect sized breasts, womanly curves, and hips I could quite happily grab on to.

I imagine most men are fucking her in their minds already, and they haven't even seen her face yet.

She manages to command attention without even doing anything. But when she starts to lift her head, she absolutely has my complete focus. I look at her lips first. Plump and a deep red. Next is her cheekbones, accentuating her face. And then I meet her eyes and my whole fucking world shifts.

Grey, stormy eyes that find mine straight away. Eyes that I looked into many times before as I fucked her, made love to her, told her how she had my heart. Eyes that show no fear, eyes that no longer look broken. Paige fucking Daniels. Miss Roderick. My kryptonite.

Chapter Three
Paige

There he stands.

Joey fucking Valentine, thirty-three years old and still the most handsome bastard I've ever laid my eyes on with his black hair perfectly styled, cut short but still long enough to be able to run your fingers through.

The man that broke my heart, and the one that will be fucking begging me for mercy in the near future.

I take no prisoners, and he's going to wish that he had never fucking met me.

Rule number one of the underworld. Trust no one.

I know how respected he is here. I know how he reigns fucking supreme amongst all of the other criminals in this room.

But I also know that I am here to take his crown. To replace him as the top dog.

I'm not that far behind him as it is, and I have managed to take everything that I have by staying hidden.

He should be fucking scared, as should every other person in this room.

I'm not one to regret. My heart shows no compassion. I have nothing to lose. And that makes me the most dangerous of them all.

His ice blue eyes flicker with recognition for a second before it disappears and his guard slides into place. If I hadn't known Joey before now, then I would never have noticed it, but whether he likes it or not, I know him better than he knows himself. I studied that motherfucker for years before he eradicated me from his life.

Friends first, lovers later.

And he will be the one screaming like a little bitch in the end.

I allow my eyes to roam around the room. Every person in here is staring at me. A small smile pulls at my lips.

Yes, fuckers. I'm here. This is me, and none of you are going to get in my goddamn way.

I hold my head high, chin tilted up as I start to address the room.

"Good evening, gentlemen," I say before adding, "And ladies." I nod to the three other women in this room. Each one of them nods back at me, their focus solely on me. Not many women make it in this world, so the ones that do already gain a little respect from me. That's not to say that they have my trust, because not many do.

I notice that the men haven't brought their significant others with them tonight. I know that every single one of them, apart from Joey, has a wife, and that the majority also have a mistress, or two, on the side. *Fucking assholes.*

"I know that you will all have been wondering who Miss Roderick is, and now, here I stand before you." I hold my arms out at the sides, proud of the fucking warrior that I have become. A few murmurs break out, but the silence soon resumes as they all wait with baited breath for my next words.

"I came into this world with nothing." I start hard, draw them in, make them think they have a way in with me, and then fucking cut them at the throat.

"Worked my way up from the gutter. You've heard the stories, and I can assure you that they are all real." Make them think I have nothing to hide. Give them more than they bargained for.

"I called you all here tonight because I believe that you all deserve to know who you are dealing with. Money is why we are here. Business dealings that will push our names to the top of the chain." My eyes flit to Joey's, and I can see that his jaw is clenched, a sign that he is annoyed, feels threatened, and that he plans to tear apart the person making him feel this way. Good. *Come at me, baby, and I'll be sure to bite back just as fucking hard.*

"But tonight is not about business." A pause for effect. "Tonight is about you all seeing what I wanted you to. Me. Paige Roderick in the flesh." I hold my hands out wide. *Take a good fucking look, boys, because I am about to play you harder than anyone ever has.*

I look to the nearest waitress and wave them over. They scurry to me quickly, keeping their head bowed, never making eye contact.

I take a glass of champagne from their tray and raise the glass in the air. Everyone in the room follows me in raising theirs. Everyone except for Joey. I smirk.

"Tonight is about drinking and having a good time. Tomorrow is the time to play, gentlemen," I finish with a wink at no one in particular as the men around me let out low laughter. I don't address the ladies with my comment because they need to know I overpower them, no fucking questions asked. The fact that they have also raised their glasses and haven't challenged me shows that they have heard about me. About what I do to those who ignore me and don't follow orders.

I take a sip of the champagne and notice that Joey is still stood there, frozen on the spot, like a goddamn statue.

I like to think it's because he is stunned, silenced and fucking seething. I can only hope that it is all three.

I'm ready for you, baby. Let the games begin.

Chapter Four
Joey

I'm a pro at schooling my reactions. I've had years of practice, and I have never been more grateful for that than I am right now.

Paige fucking Daniels, or Paige Roderick as she is now called, has completely shocked me, but I will never allow anyone to see that. Especially her.

She saunters her way over to me, looking every inch the fucking bitch that she has been portrayed to be. Long legs that stride towards me and eyes that sparkle with mischief. Damn. If I weren't a cold-hearted bastard, I'd be claiming her in front of all these fuckers right here, right now. But I am cold-hearted. No warmth left. An everlasting reminder of my time in the underworld.

A time that was coming to an end, but Miss Roderick just changed the motherfucking game.

I've been planning my escape from this life for the last three years, and all she had to do was show her face for me to start thinking about how I don't want to go anywhere. *Fuck. Don't be such a goddamn pussy, Valentine. This bitch doesn't rule your heart. Not anymore.*

"Mr Valentine," Paige says as she stops in front of me, hands on her hips, feet apart, completely aware of all her surroundings.

"Miss *Roderick*," I reply, my voice low. One of her eyebrow's quirks up, and damn if it doesn't make her look more fuckable than she did a second ago.

"Pleasure to meet you," she says as she holds her hand out for me to shake. Not the usual protocol, but nothing she has done has been the norm. She stayed hidden for fuck's sake, and that makes her more dangerous than most.

I look at her hand for a second before my eyes settle back on hers, and I can see the challenge there. Fucking game on.

Her hand moulds against mine, and fuck if the feel of her skin on mine after all of these years doesn't make my dick twitch in my pants. I'm a ruthless motherfucker for sure, but I'm still a dude with a dick, and she's previously had mine in her mouth, so I know how good that shit feels.

Her smirk has me pulling away before she can.

I am aware that others are watching our exchange. The alpha and the unknown. Valentine and Roderick. Two top dogs, but only one spot available.

I place my hands in my trousers pockets and stand tall. My right hand man, Raymond, is stood to the side of me, keeping watch, making sure no one gets close. But he didn't stop her from walking over here, and maybe he should have. She's a threat. Not to my position of power, but to me personally. A face I never thought that I would see again. A ghost that has come back to haunt me. The biggest threat that I have ever faced.

I mask my thoughts behind dead eyes. I refuse to let her see the effect she is having over me. She needs to remain at arm's length. Never let her close. Never let her in. Never show her my hand. Let her think that she is running the game.

"I believe we have some business to discuss," she says, her eyes never wavering.

"And what business might that be?"

She lets out a little chuckle as if she thinks that I am stupid. I am anything but.

"Come on, Mr Valentine, don't play coy with me," she starts, stepping closer, leaving an inch of space between us. "You know that unfinished business is always the best kind." Her voice is low, almost a whisper, but her words hit me with force. Like a fucking blow to the chest. Unfinished business. Always messy. Always satisfying. Retribution in its best form.

Now it's my turn to step forward, bend my head and place my lips by her ear.

"I *never* leave business unfinished, Paige."

She moves her head back slightly, her nose almost touching mine.

"No? Then how come I'm stood in front of you, Mr Valentine? How come I walked in here and commanded this room like the fucking queen that I am?" she says, smugness lacing her tone. "I'm your unfinished business, Joey, and make no mistake, I never lose."

She doesn't wait for my response before turning her back on me and walking away. I watch as she holds her head high and marches through the men lining the room. Not one of them try to approach her. If she were a man, the lines would have been drawn, and he would have been challenged within seconds. But stick a high ranking woman in here and all the men turn into pussies.

Paige Roderick just put the challenge in place, and fuck if I'm not up for the shots to be fired.

Chapter Five
Paige

I walk over to Donovan who stands to the side of the room.

"Talk to me, Don," I say as I stand in front of him, his face rigid, jaw tight. He's a hunk of a man. Tall, dark green eyes, light brown hair shaved close to his head, broad shoulders and arms that rival that of a heavy weight boxer, not to mention buns of fucking steel.

He's been with me the whole time. My right hand man, and the guy that helped drag me out of the gutter three years ago, yet I still wouldn't trust him with my life. I trust him as much as I need to, and that's as good as its going to get.

"Montell ain't giving it up, Paige," he says quietly, making sure no one around us can hear him.

"Motherfucker," I say on a breath. "He say why?"

"Apparently he doesn't have the cash," Donovan says, his teeth clenched together in anger. I know that Donovan would take out anyone that I asked him to. Hell, he's done it before now without me asking. All I need to do is give him the nod and the world will be rid of one more parasite, but I think I need to deal with Montell myself.

"No cash and the fact that he thinks dealing with a woman makes me a soft touch," I say with a shake of my head. "Stupid, stupid man."

"Couldn't agree more, boss."

"Don't kiss my ass, Donovan," I say as I glare at him. He may have my back, but I don't need him to try and suck up to me. He's proved his worth. "Where is he now?"

"At his digs with Bray and Tony," Donovan informs me. Bray and Tony, two of the boys that do my dirty work so that I can keep my hands clean. Gone are the days of me needing to take care of business myself, but sometimes it can be fun. Gives me a thrill. Reminds me of how I got here.

"They got him covered?" I need to know what I'm going to be walking into.

"All alone, boss," Donovan confirms.

"Well, I guess it's time to leave the party," I say, not at all bothered that I am leaving so early. I came here to do one thing, and that was to let Joey know that I'm no fucking pushover. Mission accomplished, and on to the next.

"You want me to call Miles and have him be at your place?" Donovan asks.

"No. Miles doesn't need to know about this." Miles is one of my drug runners. The main man who makes me the most money. The big daddy, supplying the low lives with all that they need. He usually accompanies me to see the ones that won't pay up. But tonight I'll allow him a breather. Just for tonight mind, tomorrow I'm going to be kicking his ass for supplying an asshole that claims he can't pay.

"Make sure that Rome and Trevor are there though." Two more of my boys.

"On it," Donovan says as he whips his phone out of his pocket and sends messages to them both. I lead us out of the room, ignoring the curious glances from the people I pass and not giving a fuck what they might be thinking.

I came here, made myself known, showed my face, and hopefully made Joey want to fall on his ass. Time will tell, but they would all be stupid to cross me.

I'm not a boss bitch for nothing.

***

26

"So, Montell. Tell me, what makes you think that you can take my merchandise and not pay?" I say as I enter the room and see that he is sat on a chair, arms tied behind him, feet tied to the chair legs. I nod to Bray for him to take the gag out of Montell's mouth.

"I... I don't have the money," Montell says as the beads of sweat run down his face.

I let out a callous laugh. "Do you think that is a good enough excuse?" I say as I stand in front of him, arms by my sides, feet inches from his.

"I'm sorry, but it's all I can say," he replies. Fucking idiot. "I got kids, I got bills to pay, and my wife—"

"Ah, yes, the lovely Tonya," I say before he can finish his sentence. His eyes go wide as if he didn't expect me to know fuck all about him. I make it my business to know who I'm dealing with. "The wife that waits at home for you, worrying about whether you will make it through another day or if you might overdose and die a shitty death."

Montell has the decency to look ashamed, hanging his head.

"The wife that has no idea about your dirty little trips to the strip club where you get your kicks," I continue, and his eyes fly back up to mine. I smirk.

"Tell me, Montell. Do you think that because I am a woman that you can fucking side step me?" I say, my voice harder, my eyes burning into his.

"N... No, Miss." Fucking stuttering. Weak-ass pussy.

"Do you think that you can get out of what is owed to me?"

"I just need a little more time—"

"You've had time," I say, cutting him off. "In fact, you've had too much fucking time." Something I will be talking to Miles about tomorrow.

"Please, I can get it, I can, I just—"

"Need more time, you've already said." My voice doesn't waver. I've dealt with bigger assholes than this. Showed them who was boss. Now I'm about to give Montell an education in why it is important to never, ever piss me the fuck off.

"Tony," I say, holding my hand out, no other words needed. Tony picks up the petrol can beside the door. Donovan brought it in when we arrived, placed it down without Montell noticing. Rome and Trevor are outside, covering the front door. Bray and Tony stand behind Montell, and Donovan stands behind me. They all know what I'm capable of, and they all know not to cross me. Such a shame that Montell didn't get the memo.

Tony hands me the petrol can, and I take the cap off, stepping closer to Montell, wafting the can under his nose so he can smell the fumes.

"Smells good, doesn't it?" I say as he looks at me with wide eyes. "Now imagine how good it will smell when it starts to burn." With that, I start to pour the liquid on Montell, slowly, over his head. He starts squealing like a little bitch, but that only shows how fucking weak he is. There is no place for weakness in this world. The minute you show it is the minute you get hurt. A hard lesson to learn, but one that will put you in good stead for the future.

I empty the entire can over his head before dropping the container to the floor, the sound echoing around the room.

The box of matches is handed to me by Bray. I take them, my eyes never leaving Montell and Bray steps back into place, like a good boy.

The sound of Montell whimpering is annoying. He could at least have some self-respect and shut the fuck up. Take

28

his punishment like a man, but I guess that he would have to have been a man in the first place instead of some little bitch who can't take responsibility for his ignorance.

I crouch down, my eyes level with Montell's. The fear in them makes me feel powerful, reminds me that I am no longer the one that has to be frightened.

"Now, Montell, you have one last chance to hand over the four thousand pounds that you owe me, or I end your life, make you suffer, leave the remains for your wife to find." I don't fuck around, and I mean every word.

"Please—"

"The time for apologies has gone."

"My kids—"

"Probably wouldn't fucking remember you for being anything other than a dirty druggie," I say. His kids are sixteen and fourteen. Old enough to know what their father is. A fucking waster.

"They need me," he whispers.

"And I need my money," I say deadpan.

I bet his heart is beating ten to the fucking dozen. His adrenaline through the God damn roof.

"I haven't got it," he replies, and then tries to plead with me some more.

"Wrong fucking answer, asshole," I say as I take a match out of the box and light it, the flame flickering, signalling the end of Montell's life. "Any final words?"

"You won't do it," Montell says, attempting to call my bluff.

I laugh at his stupidity. "Don't ever fucking doubt me," I snarl as I move the match closer to his body. Montell screams, tears run down his face and I move the match closer. I do it slowly, drawing out his distress for thinking that I won't do it. I've done worse. This is nothing. Minor stuff. It's just a lesson. One I bet he wishes he hadn't showed up for.

I am millimetres from touching the match to his clothes when he squeals.

"It's under the floorboard, over there, by the bed," he says as he nods his head towards the general direction that he is referring to. The fact that this man can't provide more than a bedsit for his wife and kids shows how much he values his drug habit over his family. Worst kind of human. Selfish.

I don't need to tell Donovan to check. He knows the drill.

A few tense seconds tick past, the match burning down closer to my fingers.

"It's all here, boss," Donovan says.

Now I have a choice. Take the money and give this fucker one last chance at life or burn him and this shit hole to the ground. Decisions, decisions.

"You know, Montell, it must be your lucky day," I say as I blow the match out and throw it on the floor. Montell breathes an audible sigh of relief, but his body continues to tremble. It probably will for days, and he will probably spend the remainder of his life looking over his shoulder. It will only be a matter of time before he gets himself killed. Either the drugs or his next dealer will kill him.

"Don't ever fuck with me, do you understand?" I say and Montell nods his head frantically.

"Don't ever think that you will get drugs from one of my boys again. If I so much as see you sniffing around, I will end you, do you understand?" Another nod, more tears running down his face. I don't know whether that's because of my threat, or because he's got to find another dealer that will allow him to buy now, pay later. Either way, my work here is done.

I stand tall, turn around and leave the shitty bedsit, Donovan behind me, Bray and Tony still with Montell.

I had my fun, and now they get to have theirs. Montell won't get away with just petrol being poured over him. Bray and Tony will show him what the consolation prize is.

I walk outside of the run-down apartment block, Rome and Trevor either side of the main doors, and go to my waiting car. My driver, a big beefy motherfucker called Johnboy, opens my car door, silently nods as I slide into the back seat. Donovan slides in behind me, and Johnboy gets back in the driver seat.

"Not a bad day at the office," Donovan says as he hands over the four thousand pounds.

"If Miles had his shit together he would never have let the debt get that high," I say, putting the money on the seat beside me. No fucker is going to steal it.

"He seems to be letting shit slip," Donovan says. I remain silent, but I have already noticed that Miles is letting the debts rack up higher than usual.

"He'll learn," is all I say, Donovan chuckling at my words.

They all learn eventually.

Chapter Six
Joey

"This is fucking bullshit," I shout as I throw the contract on the desk in front of me. A new contract for a new drug deal. One where I take all of the risks and end up with fuck all profit.

"Is this a motherfucking joke?" I yell at Raymond, one of my most trusted people.

"No, Joey, it's not," Raymond replies, his shoulders drooping. Raymond has been with me for the last eight years. Pretty much guided me from the moment that I took the reins. He was my father's right hand man. Watched me grow up. Came to Sunday dinner. Looked out for me when my father died.

"Who's fucking with us, Ray?" I ask him the question, needing to know who is undercutting me and bringing my profit down to the lowest it's ever been.

"Miss Roderick," he says, face straight, lips pulled into a thin line.

"How?"

"I don't know."

"Not good enough."

"I know, Joey. I know it's not good enough, but aside from making the bare fucking minimum, there is no other way that she can undercut us," Raymond tells me. "Ronnie Masters won't take any other deal, not with Miss Roderick's on the table. We either go lower or he moves ship."

"And all of the fucking years of loyalty we've shown him? The protection we have given him when it has been needed?" I say.

"Totally irrelevant," Raymond says, but we both know that there is no such thing as irrelevant in this world. Not unless the word refers to a person about to be put into a body bag. We also both know that Ronnie Masters needs to be taught a lesson in respect. Nobody ships out on me. Fucking no one.

"Why now? Why is she doing this now?" I ask out loud, more to myself than to Raymond.

"You got beef with her, Joey?" Raymond asks me, and I freeze for a second before I start pacing up and down my office.

"I've only just fucking met her, Ray." I have no desire to tell him about how Paige was my secret sanity all those years ago. My secret, and now the one trying to be my fucking downfall.

"You sure about that?" he asks, and I stop, turning to face him, my stare hard, unnerving.

"You questioning me?" I ask, my tone showing how pissed off I am at having to ask that in the first place. No fucker questions me.

"Of course not, Joey. I apologise," Ray says as he holds his hands up in surrender before lighting up a cigarette that he just pulled from his jacket pocket. He offers me one, and I take it, lighting the fucker up and taking a deep inhale. The smoke fills my lungs and I exhale, my anger threatening to boil over.

"Set me up a meeting with Ronnie. I want that fucker to tell me to my face that he's hopping ship."

"Done," Raymond says, flicking his ash into the crystal ashtray that sits on my desk.

"Then get Miss Roderick to agree to a meeting. No matter what it takes."

"Okay, Joey. I'll do some digging, see what else I can find out."

"You should have done that already," I tell him, pissed that she's managed to sweet-talk one of my biggest clients away from me.

With a wave of my hand I dismiss Raymond and turn to look out of the floor to ceiling windows that run along the back wall of my office, offering me a view of nothing but countryside.

I hear the door click closed behind Raymond and I continue to smoke my cigarette.

"I'm your unfinished business, Joey, and make no mistake, I never lose." Paige's words resound in my head.

Unfinished business, a woman scorned.

The worst fucking kind.

*** *** ***

I'm sitting in the back room of an upscale restaurant, waiting for Miss Roderick to show her face.

She agreed to a meeting. Set it up pretty quickly.

Five hours ago I found out that she had undercut me on a deal, and now I sit, ready to face her and ask what the fuck she thinks she is doing.

I sip my glass of mineral water. No alcohol has touched my lips. I need my wits about me, my complete focus and concentration on what is to come.

We're both at the head of our operations, and we're both aware that we need to be on alert.

Raymond waits outside of this room for me, along with Gary, Nate and Leon. Pascal and Simon wait outside in separate cars. I take no chances. It's how I got to where I am today.

A door on the other side of the dark room opens, and there she is, looking every inch as fucking gorgeous as she did at the party she threw. The one where she revealed herself to the whole damn underworld, or as good as. The one where she showed me that she made it, got to a place of power, and sure as shit has men falling at her feet.

A motherfucking goddess.

Walking towards the table that I sit at, she is wearing skin-tight, dark blue jeans, a white long-sleeved top that hugs every enticing curve of her body, and sexy-ass black boots that I would demand that she kept on whilst I fucked her, hard. Her long blond hair is pulled back, away from her face, allowing me to see every feature. Dark make-up lines her eyes, and her lips shimmer against the dim lighting of the room. Her grey eyes give nothing away. She's got her guard up, and I'm going to have so much fun breaking the damn thing down.

"Mr Valentine," she says as she takes a seat opposite me, crossing her legs.

"Miss Roderick," I reply with a nod of my head. I would have called her Miss Daniels, but I'll save that for when I really want to get to her. She changed her name for a reason, and I bet that reason has something to do with me. Call it intuition, call it self-righteousness, call it whatever the fuck you like. She was a Daniels when I first met her, but she is far from a Daniels now. The woman sat in front of me grew a back-bone and fought with the best of us. And now, she's about to make her move.

"So, here we are," she says, sitting back and holding her hands out either side of her. Like a fucking queen. Damn, I'm going to have to knock her down a peg or two. She can't run against me. I won't allow it.

"I guess so."

"All alone for the first time in three years," she says, a smirk playing on her lips.

"Alone? You mean you haven't got a hoard of men waiting outside of this room, keeping watch, listening out to see if they need to come in here and save you?" I say sarcastically.

She chuckles lightly, and it does things to my dick.

"Come on, Joey, you know that I have no need to worry about being on my own with you," she says, her eyes twinkling with mischief.

"You sure about that?" I challenge her, raising my eyebrows.

"I know you, Joey," she says, her voice low.

"You knew me back then, but you don't know me now," I assure her. It's been three fucking years, I am not the person that I was back then.

"You're still the same guy."

"And how the fuck would you know?" I bite back.

"I know more than you think."

"Well, why don't you enlighten me?" I say, intrigued as to what she thinks she knows about me.

"I know that you have a pocket knife tucked into your sock, a gun at your back and another one in the inside pocket of your jacket. Not to mention the guys waiting outside of this room and the two cars parked outside with your getaway drivers." She looks more than satisfied with her answer, and I have to be honest, it pisses me the fuck off.

"I also know that you're here to speak to me about Ronnie Masters, and you're here to try and decipher my game plan."

"None of those things are a secret."

"Maybe not, but the fact that you are planning to escape this life is," she says and fuck if I'm not thrown for a loop. No one knows about my escape plan. No one. So how the hell does she know?

I keep my face straight, not reacting.

"Tell me, Joey. If you're so intent on leaving this life behind, why the fuck do you care whether Ronnie Masters takes a shipment from me instead of from you?" she asks, leaning back in her chair and crossing her arms over her chest, pushing her breasts a little higher.

I take a moment to digest her answer. I need to go careful here. She knows my biggest secret and she hasn't wasted any time in letting me know.

I sip my water, wetting my mouth. I show no sign of feeling intimidated, because I am the motherfucking king around here. Top dog. The main man, and I have no intention of becoming Paige Roderick's bitch.

"For starters, I have no idea where you get your intel from, but I can assure you that it is way off. And as for Ronnie Masters, I just want to know how you're making any kind of money from the obviously shitty deal you're getting, not to mention that you're treading in my territory."

I close my mouth and wait. I'm on high alert, looking for any signs of weakness in her armour. Currently, there are none.

"Your territory?" she questions. "What makes it yours?"

"I've been running these streets for the last eight years. You do not get automatic rights to come here and attempt to take over."

"Why not? You always liked a challenge, Joey, and you don't get to decide how this game plays out," she replies, taunting me, goading me, fucking with me.

"If you're gonna play with the big boys then make sure you know what you're doing, Paige. It takes more than riding some guys dick to get to the top of the chain," I reply, trying to piss her off.

"You think I got here by sucking cock, Joey?"

"I said riding, but either would work on a weak man."

The bitter laugh she lets out irks me.

"Are you weak, Joey?" she says, licking her lips.

"You know better than anyone that I am in no way weak."

"Oh, I remember, baby," she purrs and my dick twitches again. It's the first time in years it has so much as tingled when a woman has been near me, and it just had to be fucking Paige that brought the damn thing to life.

I clench my jaw and her eyes light up as she notices. I try to relax, but fuck, she's got me all tied up. Joey Valentine, fucked up over a woman. Never thought the day would come. But here we are, Paige and Joey, a blast from the past, and one that I want underneath me. We always had a crazy attraction and for me, it seems that hasn't fucking changed.

Paige stands up and walks around the table, slowly, until she is standing beside me. Her arm reaches out and she places her hand on the back of my chair, the other on the table in front of me. She bends down, placing her lips by my ear.

"Tell me, Joey. Do you remember how good we were together? Do you remember how I screamed your name, how I doted on your every word and how you told me you loved me?"

Her words. Her scent. Her plump lips so close have me clenching my fists.

"Do you remember how you promised me the world, only to throw me away like fucking trash a few days later?" she continues, pushing every single button inside of me.

"Do you remember how I begged you, pleaded with you to let me stay, let me be yours?"

Fuck. Of course I remember. The look in her eyes from that day has never left me.

"Well, baby," she says, running her tongue along my ear lobe. "It's payback time, and I'm here to teach you a fucking lesson." Her words are laced with anger and hatred but fuck if they don't get my blood pumping just a little bit faster.

"So you want revenge?" I ask the question, even though it's fairly obvious that she wants nothing more than to watch me fall.

"You catch on quick, Joey," she says, mocking me. "And let me tell you, you are going to be the one thrown into the gutter. You will be the one down on your knees, and you will be the one fucking begging me to give you one more chance."

Her words push me, they ignite a fire inside of me, and before I know it, I have her pinned against the wall, one hand holding her hip, the other wrapped lightly around her neck. And still there is nothing on her face but a smirk.

"Still like it rough, huh, baby?" she says, and all I want to do is take her, fuck her, and make her mine.

She had a hold over my heart before, but now... Now I can't let her in. I can't give into her, and I can't open myself up to her again. I'm too smart to fall in love. Learnt the hard way. Paid my dues. Pushed my fucking pain to the side and trampled over any motherfucker that stood in my way. Yeah, Paige fucking Roderick broke me before, and there is no way that she will do it again. I may have been the one to pull the plug on us, but she took my goddamn heart and ran with it. It's not been the same since. Scarred, black and fucking lifeless. The heart is just an organ, makes the blood go round. There is no room for love. Love is dangerous, love is stupid, and love is the root of all fucking evil.

"You have no idea what you're getting yourself into," I warn her as I push my body against hers. She lets out a low groan and I have to silently send signals to my dick to stand the fuck down.

"Oh, I do, Joey, and make no mistake, I will take you down, I will reign supreme, and you will end up as nothing but a pawn to your queen. I came here to play, and the games have only just begun," she says in a sickly sweet voice.

I take a moment, letting my eyes roam over her face, committing every part of this moment to memory.

That groan she let out, I know it was the real deal. A quick flash of want in her eyes showed me her weakness. Me. I'm her fucking kryptonite, and I know exactly how to fuck up her game.

The battle lines have been drawn, and I will remain the king of the playing field.

I step back, adjust my suit jacket and smile.

"I await your next move, Paige. Don't leave me hanging." It's the last thing I say before I turn my back on her and walk out of the door.

Chapter Seven
Paige

Ugh. Fucking Joey. Getting in my face. Touching my body. Making me remember what we were like together.

He left the room a few minutes ago, and now I sit back at the table, Donovan sat in the seat that Joey was in, both of us with a shot glass in our hands and a bottle of tequila sat in the middle of us, waiting to be poured.

"So?" Donovan asks, waiting for me to fill him in on my meeting with Joey. He's going to be waiting a long fucking time.

"So what?"

"What went down just now?" he asks, and I feel my irritation spike.

"Since when do you question me about what the fuck went down with anyone?" I fire back at him, my eyes trained on his.

"I'm not questioning you, Paige."

"Well, it sure sounds like you are."

"Don't mistake my worry for fucking nosiness, Paige," Donovan replies, his eyes hard.

"Worry? Why the hell would you need to worry?" I ask him.

"I've known you for the last three years, pulled you from the fucking streets, helped you get where you are today. Yet, I've never seen you as unnerved as I do now," Donovan says, straight-faced.

He watched me interact with Joey at the party, and he's watching me now, assessing me, finding a chink in my armour.

I need to shut down this shit, and quick. If Donovan is questioning me, then it won't be long before others do.

"Unnerved? You think that I'm unnerved?" I say as I sit forward in my seat, keeping my face blank, needing to make Donovan back the fuck up. "There is not one bone in my body that is unnerved, Donovan. I am in control, I am playing the fucking part that I need to. All you need to worry about is whether you can pull off your part in the motherfucking game. Joey goddamn Valentine isn't going to know what's hit him by the time I'm finished. We are going to ride this wave and come out on top. No one is going to stop me. No one is going to dissuade me, and no one is going to sit in front of me and question my fucking actions. Do I make myself clear?" I don't back down. Far from it. I am here to rule, and I will be the fucking queen of the underworld. Every person will know who I am, regardless of whether I want to ride Joey's dick or not.

"Crystal, boss," Donovan says with a smile on his face. This is how he knows me. Raw, honest, and ready to take on anybody. He doesn't know about my history with Joey. No one does. They don't need to. And if they ever found out that I used to be in love with the guy, it would completely ruin all that I have built.

I've said before that love makes you weak, and once others see it, you're screwed.

My guard will remain high.

Joey will not make his way into my heart again.

I am a ruthless woman, and I want to be at the top of the chain.

Men will bow to me. They will fear me.

I will reign supreme.

And tonight, I started the ball rolling by calling Joey's bluff. I saw the slight flicker in his eyes when I mentioned him wanting to leave this life behind. A lucky guess on my part, and one that I now know is absolutely fucking true. He forgets that I used to know him, he forgets that I used to be able to see deep inside his soul and get answers before he ever told them to me. He never said anything out loud, but his ice blues always gave him away. The subtle eye rolls, the stifled groans and the tension that would radiate throughout his body when he was called away from me. I clocked it all, and my lucky guess just solidified the answer I always knew. He wants out. My plan to take his crown may be easier than I thought.

Donovan opens the bottle of tequila, pours the liquid into the shot glasses and pushes one towards me.

I lift my glass up, Donovan does the same.

"Here's to taking down Joey Valentine," Donovan says as he raises his glass in the air.

I nod my head, eyes hard, lips in a straight line.

Yes, here's to taking down Joey fucking Valentine.

Chapter Eight
Paige

"What the fuck is this?" I ask as I wave the invitation around.

"Well, I'm gonna take a guess and say that it's something that you're not happy about," Donovan says as he sits on the seat on the other side of my desk. "Who's it from?"

"Joey Valentine."

"Really?" Donovan says his eyebrows raised.

"An invitation to his new club opening on Saturday night," I tell him.

"I see." Donovan scratches his jaw seeming unfazed that Joey has requested my presence at his damn club.

"I basically tell the guy that I want to take his fucking crown and he invites me to one of his events."

"He's cooking something up," Donovan says, confirming what I already know.

"Damn straight he is. But what exactly? I mean, I am his direct competition. I am ready to hand his ass to him, so why the hell would he want me there?" I ask out loud.

"To show everyone that he is in control," Donovan says.

"To make sure that I know my place," I add.

"Exactly."

"To try and show the underworld elite that he is still the top dog."

"Without a doubt," Donovan says. "Make no mistake that Joey will be wanting to cement his status. You came out of nowhere, stayed hidden for a long time, unveiled yourself and then let him know that you want what he has. A man like Joey will always have an ulterior motive, Paige."

I swivel from side to side on my seat, thinking Donovan's words over.

Of course Joey will want to show me that he can't be taken down.

Of course he will want to show every other fucker in that room that he is going nowhere.

"Well," I start, sitting forward in my chair, bracing my elbows on my desk and resting my chin on my hands, "I guess I'm just going to have to put my secret moves into play sooner than planned."

"And what secret moves is that, boss?" Donovan asks me.

I smile and shake my head a little. "Oh, Don, don't you know by now that I have a certain way of getting men to listen?"

Donovan chuckles as he registers what I'm saying. Granted, my certain way is usually threatening them until they cave like the pussies that they are, but with Joey, I'm going to use a different approach. No need to tell Donovan that though. It's none of his God damn business.

It's not going to be easy, but then, nothing that I have ever done has been easy.

And with mine and Joey's history, it shouldn't take me too long to crack his exterior.

I'm not in the habit of using my womanly gifts to cloud a man's judgement, but on this occasion, I'm going to have some fun whilst doing it.

I'm about to up the ante. Raise the stakes.

Make Joey think that he is wearing me down.

Make Joey think that my heart is letting him in.

And then when I have him where I want him, I'm going to cut him at the throat.

Chapter Nine
Joey

The club is packed, a successful opening night so far. It's the third club that I have opened within the town, but this one is exclusive. Only the elite get in here. All the fucking gangster wannabes can go party at one of my other spots. Club Valentine is a private members club, and most of them are only here because I invited them.

Of course there are a couple of men here who have brought their mistresses with them, but those mistresses won't utter a word about this place to anyone. They would be too damn scared to. Hanging off of the arm of some of the toughest bastards around is seen as a privilege to some, and they certainly won't want to give up their fully furnished apartments and monthly spending allowance.

The club is heavily guarded. I want these people to feel like they can relax here. The more they are comfortable, the more they will come here and the more they will line my pockets.

The main room has a stage area to the back of the room, straight across from the bar. Stools line the bar area, booths run along the far left wall, and the dance floor is in front of the stage.

The deejay booth is set at the left side of the stage, and a cage hangs either side of the stage for when the girls go in there to dance. And by girls, I mean the ones that have been hired to work here, to please the eyes of the men that will be acquainting this place.

Has no effect on me, but if it helps bring in the business, I'm all for it.

There is an upstairs where you will find tables that are well-spaced, so no one feels cramped, and a small bar to save anyone having to bother to walk down to the main room to get a drink.

Then we have the rooms out the back. One for the staff, one for the club manager, one for my own personal use, and the room where deals and poker games are played in the basement below, which is soundproof, just in case any motherfucker tries to start shit and it needs to be dealt with.

I stand on the top floor, my hands braced against the balcony that overlooks the dance floor. A couple of people are using the tables behind me, talking quietly, but I have no interest in them right now. The only person I have interest in is the one that just walked in.

Paige fucking Roderick.

The motherfucking goddess, stood there in tight leather pants that look like they're painted on, a black vest top and studded black boots. Her hair is hanging in loose waves around her face, and she wears red lipstick that stands out from a mile away. Absolute perfection. Such a shame I'm going to have to kick her ass to the curb again, eventually. I can't have people thinking that she has an effect on me, but I can have some fun before I crush her dreams of taking over my spot.

I invited her here tonight so that I can put my plan into action. Reel her in, make her want me, then push her away harder than I did before.

She thinks she's dangerous, but she's got fucking nothing on me.

I see her right hand man, Donovan, is following closely behind her. Her invite only allowed her a plus one, but I know that she will have others waiting outside for her. She would be a fool not to, especially with all the names in here tonight.

"Boss," I hear Raymond say as he walks over and stands beside me. "Miss Roderick just arrived."

"I know." Everyone here knows that she just arrived. She commands attention without even trying.

"Want me to get her up here?" Raymond asks. He knows that I have something planned for her, but he doesn't know what exactly. Keep your cards close to your chest, never show your hand.

"Clear the floor, then invite her up."

Raymond goes to walk away but I stop him.

"Just her, not her puppet," I say, referring to Donovan.

"You got it, boss," Raymond says before he tells the other guests to move to the bottom floor, and then descends the stairs to go and tell Paige that I want to see her. I'm pretty sure she isn't going to come willingly but then, she may surprise me. Fuck knows she's done that more than once since popping back into my life.

I watch as Raymond walks over to her. She eyes him suspiciously. I smirk.

Always on her guard. Always waiting for the bomb to drop.

She's going to be waiting for a while for this bomb to detonate.

I'm going to feel her out, get in her head and make her so fucking hot for me that she won't be able to focus on anything else.

I can do that. I did it once before, I'll do it again.

Raymond starts to walk back to the stairs, and to my surprise, she follows him, her head held high. I watch her hips sway and I notice the men lusting after her as she gets to the bottom of the stairs that will lead her up to me. Raymond gestures for her to go ahead before he looks up at me and nods. I nod back, and Raymond stands at the bottom of the stairs, Antonio joining him to stop any one else trying to come up here.

The music pumps through the sound system, the bass gently vibrating as I sit down at one of the tables and wait for Paige to emerge.

When she reaches the top of the stairs she looks around, assessing her surroundings before her eyes lock with mine.

I stop the smile from spreading across my face as she saunters towards me.

Fucking stunning. Fucking ruthless. And about to be fucking mine.

"Well, Mr Valentine, the invitation didn't say anything about a private party," she says, stopping at the table and taking the seat opposite me.

"If it had, would you have still come?" I ask her, my eyes boring into hers.

She smirks. "You know me, Joey, always curious."

"You know what curiosity did, don't you?"

"Killed the cat," she answers before adding, "But I'm no cat."

"No? Then what are you?"

"I'm the motherfucking viper, baby," she answers, and this time I can't stop the smile from spreading over my face.

"Yes you are," I say quietly, but she hears me, even with the music pumping away.

"What's the matter, Joey? Scared I'll bite?" she taunts me.

"Not at all. In fact, I can't wait for you to sink your teeth in," I reply. Her eyes give her away briefly, igniting with lust. She shuts it down just as quickly as it came, but I saw.

I see you, baby, you can't hide from me.

"So," I begin, leaning back in my chair. "What do you think of my new club?"

"It's all right," she says with a shrug of her shoulders.

"Just all right?"

She makes a show of sweeping her eyes around the room.

"It's tasteful, the music isn't bad, and I can see there are plenty of hidden corners. Tell me, is that for shady business deals or for when the customers can't control themselves and they have to have a quick grope before fucking their mistress in the back room?"

She quirks an eyebrow and I can't help the laughter that falls from my mouth.

"Do you really think that I would let people conduct themselves in that way in my club?" I question.

"I wouldn't put it past you, Joey."

Her comment annoys me and my laughter fades. It shouldn't bug me, but it does.

"I wouldn't allow anyone to be disrespected in this club, Paige, and people fucking in the corner would be just that. Disrespectful. As for the fucking in the back room, that will only be done by me, in my private room, away from the beady eyes that see everything."

"But money talks, right? The right amount would persuade you." She's goading me, trying to push my buttons. And it's fucking working.

"Is that what you do? Give up your morals for money?" Her eyes narrow on me and I take that as a win. *Yeah, baby, I can give it right back to you. Come at me, let me see what else you got.*

"I make my money without giving up anything," she says, eyes blazing. "I don't need to bow to a man to make it in this world, and I sure as hell don't open my legs to turn a profit."

"You sure about that?" I ask, baiting her. "You haven't fucked your boy Donovan? Isn't that why he's always hanging around?"

"Does that mean you fucked Raymond?"

"Touché," I reply. She knows Raymond is my right hand man, just as I know that Donovan is hers.

"Speaking of fucking," she starts, her eyes twinkling. "Where's your piece of skirt, Joey? I haven't seen one hanging around, and don't most big, bad, gangster men have a hoard of women ready to trail them around like a lost little puppy?"

"I don't like puppy dogs."

"Maybe not, but who's taking care of you, Joey? Tending to your needs, making you feel like the powerful fucking king that you are?" she says, and fuck if I don't want her to make me feel like a goddamn king right now.

"There's only ever been one woman that can handle me," I reply, my gaze fixed on her. I don't fail to notice the slight intake of her breath at my total honesty. She probably thinks that I'm messing with her, but I have never meant the words more than I do now.

"Oh yeah? What happened to her?" she asks me, even though she is fully aware of the answer to that question. But we're here to play, so play I will.

"I had to give her up, push her away, make her think that I hated her."

The silence stretches between us.

My words sinking in.

"Why?" she asks, her voice quieter than a moment ago.

"To save her."

"Pfft," she scoffs, but I can almost see the cogs turning in her head. "You don't think she could have decided for herself whether she was safe or not?"

"No, I don't."

51

"That's a cop-out and you know it," she says, her fire once again beginning to ignite.

"Maybe, but it was my truth back then, and I would do the same thing again, given the choice."

"You sure you didn't just get bored with her? Chuck her away like some rag doll, only to replace her with a newer model?" She's looking for more answers, and I have no qualms about giving them to her in this particular instance.

I lean in closer. "Trust me, Paige, there is no way in hell that she could have ever bored me. She got me, knew me, made me work for her heart, and once I claimed it, I was the happiest motherfucker alive."

"So why throw it all away? Why kick her to the curb if not for a new plaything?" she asks as she hangs on my every word. It's the most I've seen her guard drop, and at this point, I definitely know that I am the weakness in her armour. She may be a bad-ass leader, but she's still a woman, and she still wants answers to the questions I wouldn't give her answers to before.

"She wasn't ready for my world. I couldn't risk her becoming a target."

"And now?" she asks, a little breathless, probably not aware of how much I can see that she needs this for clarification of what went wrong all those years ago.

"Now?" I pause for a second, the tension around us heightening. "Now she would stand with me, beside me, be my equal."

"There is no way that you, Joey Valentine, would let a woman stand beside you," she says, her guard sliding back up.

"Don't doubt my word, Paige. I am nothing if not a fucking king in this world, and a king always needs a queen by his side."

"You wouldn't want a queen. You would want a puppet, just like these other assholes that claim they see their women as their equal. Nothing but fucking liars," she bites back, and it gets my back up. I stand, pushing my chair away, she does the same. She's trying to save face, make it seem like I haven't affected her. I side step the table and am stood in front of her before she can move away. She doesn't even flinch, lifting her chin up slightly.

"I am no liar, Paige. You know that."

"I know that you're fucking with me right now to make me weak."

I take a step towards her, she steps back, until her back is against the wall. Bad fucking planning on her part. Not so aware of her surroundings now.

"I don't want to make you weak, Paige. That fire inside of you, it makes me come alive. I'm always up for a challenge, baby, and you, you will be my greatest victory," I say, my voice low, my eyes trained on hers. I'm inches away from touching her, smashing my mouth against hers, taking what has always been mine.

"Oh, Joey, if you thought that you were going to claim me, then you are sadly mistaken," she begins. "I fell for your bullshit once before, don't think that I will make the same mistake again."

"Not bullshit, Paige. I told you, I don't fucking lie."

"And I'm just meant to take your word for it? Give in and be the good little woman that falls at your knees?"

"Absolutely not. I want you to fight me all the way, make me work, make me earn what I should never have given up in the first place," I tell her, moving my head closer, stopping with my lips just in front of hers.

"You can't earn back something that wasn't yours to begin with," she whispers, but her words hold no fucking meaning. She loved me, I know she did.

"Who's bullshitting now, Paige?" I say as I brush my lips over hers. Her whole body shudders as I move away, taking a step back.

She stands against the wall, looking more beautiful than I have ever seen. Face flushed, breathing deeply, and trying to extinguish the want in her eyes.

She doesn't say anything more as she pushes off of the wall and walks away. I don't watch her, I don't turn to get one last look before she disappears down the stairs.

Telling her the truth tonight was a risky move, but it paid off.

She still wants me.

Reeling her in may not be as hard as I first thought.

Keep her in my sights, keep her close, then pull the fucking trigger on whatever plan she has concocted.

Only trouble is, I still want her.

Always have done, probably always will.

Paige fucking Roderick. The person that could be my downfall, and the one that holds the key to my fucking heart.

Chapter Ten
Paige

"Where the fuck have you been?" I say as I look up from my desk and see Miles stood in the doorway.

I haven't heard from him since my visit to Montell. I know damn well where he has been, but I want to see if he's going to lie to my face. It wouldn't be a smart move.

"Just taking care of business, boss," Miles replies as he shuts the door and moves to the seat in front of my desk.

"Did I tell you that you could come in and sit down?" I ask.

"Oh, come on, Paige, don't be like that," Miles replies, a cocky-ass smirk on his face.

"Don't fuck with me, Miles," I retort.

"Whoa, whoa, what's bit you in the ass?" he says, seeming to forget who the fuck he is talking to. I narrow my eyes on him. I have a lot of pent up frustration, most of it coming from Joey, that I need to let out, and Miles is my number one fucking target right now.

I put the pen down that I was writing with and lean back in my chair, resting my elbows on the arms.

"Firstly, don't forget who pays you your fucking money and keeps your ass from getting into trouble. Secondly, don't ever think that you can walk in here and sit the fuck down without being invited to do so. Thirdly, you haven't answered my question. Where the fuck have you been?" My voice is dangerous and laced with anger.

Miles sits there, looking like a rabbit caught in the headlights. I let Miles get away with more than most because he brings in a good amount of money, but if he thinks I'm going to let him talk to me like I'm his bitch, he's sadly fucking mistaken.

His almost-black eyes go wide, his jaw going slack, his shoulders tense. Miles is by no means a small guy, but he knows that trying to act the fucking goat right now could very well get him a beating, and I know that he won't want his pretty face all busted up.

Miles is a looker. Blond hair that falls to his shoulders, full lips that I imagine most women wouldn't mind getting down and dirty with, biceps that are shown off with the tight tank tops that he favours, and an ass that is as peachy as they come. But he does fuck all for me. Never has, and he knows it, so pouting those plump lips at me will never work.

"Sorry, boss," he starts, less sure of himself than when he walked in here.

"So you fucking should be. Now answer the goddamn question, Miles."

"I had to go underground for a few. Had the Morgan boys looking for me," Miles says, confirming what I already know.

"And you didn't think to get a message to me? To come and fucking see me?"

"There was no time, boss."

"Bollocks. There's always time," I reply.

"Honestly, Paige, I had to get gone and quick."

"Why? What did you do to land yourself in hot water with the Morgan brothers?"

The Morgan brothers are one of the more well-known gangs that run in the same circles that we do. Aside from Joey, they are my other competition. I haven't focussed on taking anything from them just yet because they don't tread in my waters, but if they're after Miles, they are essentially after me, and that is a problem that I need to take care of.

"I fucked their sister and they found out," he says, looking anything but remorseful for bringing this shit to my doorstep.

"So, let me get this right, you fuck around with their slut of a sister, and I end up taking the fall?"

"I... It's..." he struggles to get his words out.

"Don't stutter at me, Miles. It pisses me off."

"Sorry, boss. You won't end up taking the fall, I'll sort it," he says, but I know there is no way in hell that he will be able to sort this. He fucked their sister, and there isn't any coming back from that.

"You need to tell me exactly what happened after you stuck your dick in her, Miles. What you said to her and whether you left it as unfinished business or not, before I walk my ass in on my meeting with the Morgans tomorrow afternoon," I tell him.

"You're meeting with them?"

"Did you ever doubt that I would?" I say, my voice hardening.

"No, but, this is my problem, Paige. I don't need you fighting my battles," he says, and I laugh in his face.

"Really, Miles? You felt the need to go into fucking hiding. You didn't think that it warranted giving me a call. You need me to clean this mess up for you, whether you want to admit that or not."

"I can handle it," he says, but we both know that the Morgan brothers would kill him before asking any questions. They are known for the torture that they inflict on the ones that piss them off, but they haven't had to deal with me yet. I shit all over their tactics, and if things don't go my way tomorrow, they will be the ones to find out the hard way.

"I'm going to meet with them, Miles. End of discussion."

Miles doesn't argue back. He wouldn't dare right now.

"Now, fill me in on what I need to know and then I'll tell you a little story of my own," I say, and I can see that his interest has been piqued.

"What you been up to, boss?" he asks, a hungry look in his eyes.

"All in good time, Miles. Now, get to talking."

He can sit there with his smug-ass grin for now. I get my answers and then he gets a lesson in why letting a debt rack up to four fucking grand is unacceptable.

Chapter Eleven
Paige

Three sets of eyes stare at me from across the table. Three sets of eyes that look every inch as pissed off as the vibes that they are omitting all around the room. Three sets of eyes that belong to the Morgan brothers. Larry, Bobby and Clive. All notorious for their scare tactics. All of them ready to dish out a punishment without asking questions first. All of them with their beady eyes boring into me.

They have been staring at me for the last few minutes. No words exchanged.

I'm sat here, legs crossed, head held high. I won't be the one to back down here. I've done nothing wrong, and I sure as shit won't suffer for Miles's faux fucking pas.

"So," Larry begins. Larry is the oldest brother, fifty-three years old, and the leader. "To what do we owe the pleasure of your visit?" he asks in the most sarcastic voice that I have ever heard. His creepy-ass smile does nothing to stop me cringing on the inside. He has a couple of teeth missing, skin that has been tanned a little too much during his lifetime, dull grey eyes and shoulder-length black hair that looks so greasy you could probably fry a fucking egg on it.

"No need for the sarcasm, Larry, you know why I'm here," I respond, not in the mood for the bullshit that always accompanies these brothers.

Larry's face drops, his smile turning into more of a snarl.

"You come into my place," he says, gesturing around the shitty, rundown room that we're sitting in, "And you think that you can take that attitude with me?"

I refrain from rolling my eyes. He's heard of me, he knows my rep, and that's why they have stayed the fuck away from my territory, but I guess he thinks that he can call the shots seeing as I requested this meeting. He's about to realise that no one calls the shots but me.

"Don't get ahead of yourself, Larry. Remember who you're talking to before you try and intimidate me," I reply deadpan.

Larry, very wisely, closes his mouth, his lips forming a tight line.

"Paige Roderick," Bobby pipes up and my head turns slightly to look at him. He's sat to the left of Larry, looking every inch as creepy as his brother. Same colour eyes, same long, lank, limp hair, and the one known to be the big-mouthed dipshit that hides behind Larry.

"You need to understand one thing, and one thing only. This is our turf. You came to us. You requested this meeting, so, be a good girl and play nice until we decide whether or not to blow your fucking brains out," Bobby finishes, and I can't help the smirk that spread across my face.

"Oh, Bobby, Bobby, Bobby, didn't your mother ever teach you any manners?" I reply.

"Fucking—"

"Ah ah ah," I cut him off with a waggle of my finger. "Be careful before you speak your next words, Bobby. You know as well as I do that you don't run shit around here. You may think that you're a tough guy, sat behind the table with your brothers sat beside you, but let me remind you about the deal we made when it was obvious that you couldn't run with the big boys." My voice is hard, unwavering.

People seem to forget about how the faceless woman made deals with them before she showed her true colours. The faceless woman being me, and now I'm about to stamp my authority over them once and for all.

"Need me to refresh your memory?" I ask, raising my eyebrows. None of them answer me, so I forge ahead. "Remember how you begged for my help when the Mendez guys were gonna take you down? Remember how you came crawling to my people to make sure that your whole existence wasn't blown to shit?"

It was the day that I realised that I was a someone. The Morgans were the next best thing after Joey. They had the monopoly on the drug running, and they made a big fucking mistake when they tried to take on the Mendez clan. A drug deal gone wrong, the big timers breathing down their God damn necks.

"If it weren't for me and my boys, you guys would be fifty feet under. The Mendez guys would have crushed you. I got rid of them. I saved all of your fucking assess, so don't you dare sit there and speak to me with no fucking respect."

All of them lean back in their seats, staying quiet like the good little puppets that they are. The minute that they came to Donovan and requested my help was the day that they became pawns in my game. They have stayed away from my territory because they couldn't come close. They don't have the balls to take me on, and they know it.

"You wanted my help without even knowing who I was back then, begging my boys for a meeting with me, down on your knees practically sucking their cocks." I helped them because I knew this day would come. I knew that at some point they would try to mess with me, and no fucker gets away with that. "And then you took that help without even knowing who I was, and now I'm here, in the flesh, and you don't like that you have to bow down to a woman."

I can see that my words are igniting something in them, their eyes give them away. Annoyance, anger and the fact that they are so far beneath me and they will never come out on top.

"So, I'll give you one last chance to start this conversation again, or I may just be forced to crush you myself."

My words are no threat, they're the real fucking deal.

Clive leans forward, bracing his arms on the table. He is the one that seems to create a calm around the fieriness that is his brothers. The calculating one. He watches, he waits, and then he makes his move. The most dangerous of the three, but still not a patch on me. His hair is shaved close to his head and he packs more pounds on his frame than his brothers do. He's the intimidator, but today it won't work.

"What did you come here for, Paige?" Clive asks me, his voice low and gravelly.

"Miles." It's the only answer I need to give, and I see the anger flare up in all three of them. Nostrils widening, cheeks reddening, and I'm sure their minds are picturing tearing Miles apart, limb from limb.

"I see," Clive says. "I hope you're not here to ask us to turn a blind eye to the disrespect that he has shown us."

"Absolutely not," I reply. I know they want revenge. No man in this world would let some guy hurt their family. But I also know that I need to show them that I have taken care of Miles myself.

"Then why are you here?" Bobby asks.

I turn my head slightly to look at him. "I came here to remind you of our agreement, which I have done, and I came here to inform you that Miles will no longer be sniffing around your sister."

"Damn fucking right he won't be," Larry pipes up.

"Yes, yes, Larry, I am aware that Miles has ruffled your feathers so to speak," I say with a wave of my hand. This type of shit bores me. I get no enjoyment out of dealing with this kind of thing. It makes me no money and just brings aggro to my door. If their sister hadn't been so quick to open her legs then this wouldn't be happening.

"Ruffled our feathers?" Bobby spits out. "Ruffled our fucking feathers? He's lucky to still be fucking walking."

"Pipe down, Bobby, I'm not the one that fucked her," I say, my jaw clenched at how he's directing his anger at me.

"Why you—"

"That's enough, Bobby," Clive says, raising his voice and stopping Bobby from finishing his sentence. Bobby wisely closes his mouth and glares at me.

"I can assure you that Miles has suffered, and he is very sorry for his actions." At this point, I pull out a photograph and lay it on the table, pushing it towards the Morgan brothers. They all eye it inquisitively, and Clive is the one to reach out and pick it up.

They take a few moments to look at the photo, all of them struggling not to smirk. The photo shows them what they want. It shows that Miles has been punished, beaten, bloodied and bruised. What the dumb pricks don't realise though, is that, yes there was some rough-housing, yes, I kicked his ass around the room a little, but his bruises are enhanced by my make-up skills. I wasn't going to completely fuck up my main drug runner, but I had to bring something to the table here to show the Morgan's that I don't take lightly to my boys fucking around.

"Satisfied?" I ask. I don't want to be here any longer than necessary.

"Okay. What do you want, Paige?" Clive asks, cutting to the chase, showing me that he probably is the brainier one of the three.

"I want your word that you will leave Miles alone."

"And?" Clive prompts.

"That's it," I reply, stumping all of them.

"That's it?" Bobby says before he can stop himself.

"Pretty simple, huh?" I respond, tilting my head to the side.

"Too simple," Bobby replies, and I can see him trying to figure me out. He needn't bother. I don't give anything away.

"You stay away from me and mine, and I stay away from you and yours," I say, my words loud and clear, my tone holding a threat behind them.

"Very well," Clive replies as he slides the photograph back across the table. I pick it up and place it back in the pocket of my jacket.

"Well, that concludes our business then, gentlemen," I say sweetly. Too sweetly. Gentlemen my ass. These guys are nothing but low life assholes who need a lesson in manners.

I stand from the table, I don't wait to be dismissed.

Without another word, I turn and walk away.

Chapter Twelve
Joey

"Who sent you here?" I ask as the poor excuse for a man who lies beneath me, my knee crushing his windpipe.

"Fuck you," he spits at me, I throw another punch. He groans as my fist connects with his cheek, his head slamming to the side.

"I can do this all night," I tell him. I have no intention of leaving here until I get my answers.

"I ain't telling you nothing," he says through gritted teeth.

"You know that if you don't tell me what I want to know, then the only way you're leaving here is in a body bag." I mean it. Every fucking word. I have no intention of letting this fucker live, not after Raymond found him trying to get into my private office here at Club Valentine.

"You need me," he says.

"I need nobody."

"You need to know who sent me," he goads, but fuck if I am going to let him know that he is right.

"You clearly know who I am, and you clearly know what I am capable of. I only ask you to tell me because I like to give people the benefit of their stupidity. Make no mistake, asshole, I will find out who sent you, but not before I torture you until you are begging like a little bitch to be spared."

The guy has the decency to close his mouth, his eyes widening a little.

"Now, I'll ask you one last time. Who sent you?" I say each word slowly.

He gulps, and I press my knee into his chest a little harder.

Time ticks by, and with every second that passes, his breathing becomes a little shallower. I press down again and wait.

Raymond is by the door, looking down at this fucker like the piece of trash that he is.

"Miss Roderick," he whispers.

"Speak up," I say, needing him to repeat the name again.

"Roderick," he says a little louder, even though I heard him the first time. The fucking shock that shoots through me is like nothing else. Paige? Paige sent him here?

"Why?" I ask.

"Information," he says, wheezing.

Fuck.

I release my hold on the twat and stand up, adjusting my suit jacket and tie. When I walk back outside of this door, I need to look every inch the fucking boss that I am.

Paige sent him here? What the hell does she want to know? What the fuck does she have planned?

"Boss?" Raymond says, and I give him a nod.

"Finish the job," I tell him and the smirk that spreads across Raymond's face would make you think that all his Christmases had come at once. Raymond loves nothing more than inflicting pain on disrespectful little runts.

"Wait," the guy calls out and I look down at him. Pitiful. "You're gonna let me go, right?" he asks, and now it's my turn to smirk.

I look him dead in the eyes as I respond. "Afraid not."

"But... but you said—"

"You think that you can come in here, uninvited, and try to dig up dirt on me? You think you have the right to walk back out of this room like nothing ever happened?"

"But I told you who sent me," he replies, his voice going a little higher pitched than it did a minute ago.

"So?" I say with a shrug of my shoulders.

"So, you gave me your word."

"No, I didn't, because my word means something. I told you what you wanted to hear, not what was actually going to happen."

"You son of a bitch," he says, knowing that his time on this planet is coming to an end quicker than he would have liked.

I don't bother to respond to his pathetic insult. I turn back to Raymond and he steps out of the way of the door.

"Enjoy yourself, Raymond," I say as I pull the door open and step outside. I can hear Raymond's laugh as I shut the door. That asshole in there is going to wish that he had never come here, especially once Raymond has had his fun.

I make my way through the club, ignoring anyone who tries to interact with me as I get to the exit and step outside.

"Boss," Big Danny says, falling into line beside me as I walk to my car. "You need me for anything?"

I stop when I reach my car and turn to face him. "You just stay here and keep watch. I need to pay someone a visit," I say before opening the car door and getting in. Big Danny walks back to the club and I start the engine.

I never travel alone. I always have someone with me, but tonight, with the revelation that Paige has sent someone to try and find out information on me, I need to deal with this on my own.

I may have crushed her heart once before, but that is going to feel like nothing compared to what I will do next.

Chapter Thirteen
Paige

"Paige," Donovan says as he waltzes into my bedroom.

"Well, excuse me, but haven't you heard of fucking knocking?" I ask as I pull my dressing gown tighter around my body.

"Now is not the time to focus on fucking knocking, Paige. We have a problem," Donovan replies, and I close my mouth. Donovan doesn't ever speak to me like this, or barge in on me, unless it's important. And by important, I mean that someone is either about to get dealt a lesson for whatever they have tried to do to screw me over, or we have an unexpected visitor.

"Joey Valentine," Donovan says, momentarily stumping me.

"Here?"

Donovan nods.

"Shit," I say as I quickly run to my walk-in closet and throw my dressing gown on the floor.

I pull out a knee length skirt, a white, sleeveless shirt, and a pair of black heels. Luckily, I still have my hair pinned up from earlier, and my make-up on. I have no desire for Joey to see me in anything other than boss mode.

I exit the closet and walk over to Donovan. He immediately turns and leads me from my bedroom.

"Did he say why he was here?" I ask, wondering why on earth Joey fucking Valentine would be paying me a visit at my private residence.

"No. He merely says that he isn't leaving until he speaks with you, and he looks all kinds of pissed off."

"Pfft, a pissed off Joey is nothing."

"I don't know, Paige. I mean, I know that we have dealt with some of the toughest assholes in this business, but none of them have been on the same wavelength as Joey."

I stop walking, Donovan doing the same. Turning my head to look at him, I know that my eyes are blazing.

"Joey is no more dangerous than anyone else that I have dealt with."

"I beg to differ," Donovan says before he can stop himself.

I take a step closer to him, my eyes narrowing. "Are you doubting me?"

"No, boss," Donovan replies quickly.

"You sure about that?" I question.

"Absolutely."

"Good," I reply, satisfied with his answer for now. "You know better than anyone else that I will never let anyone take my fucking crown."

"I know, boss. Sorry."

With a nod of my head I continue walking, the click of my heels echoing along the hallway.

When I reach the top of the stairs, I look down and see that Joey is stood by the front door, his stance dominant, Bray and Tony pointing their guns on him. Donovan wasn't kidding when he said that Joey looked pissed off. His jaw is clenched, as are his fists at his sides, his legs slightly parted. He looks ready for battle, and I've been waiting for this day for a long time. Guess all I need to do now is find out what has got him so rattled.

"Mr Valentine," I start as I make my way down the stairs. Joey's eyes follow every one of my movements. "To what do I owe the pleasure of your unexpected visit?" I sound like a bitch, and damn does it feel good. But you know what feels even better? The way that Joey is devouring me with his eyes like he wants to fuck my brains out and reprimand me at the same time.

I smirk at the memory of us. Together. In his bed, in the car, in the alleyway behind what used to be our favourite restaurant. We couldn't get enough of one another. Some might find it repulsive that we couldn't keep it contained to the bedroom, but fuck what they think. Joey and I were hot together, and his eyes hold the same fire that they did once before.

I reach the bottom of the stairs and come to a stop. Joey still hasn't said a word, but the flaring of his nostrils has picked up pace.

"Cat got your tongue, Mr Valentine?" I goad. Still silence. I roll my eyes. Joey has no idea how much I love a challenge nowadays. I didn't fight for what I wanted all those years ago, but now it's a different story. My heart grew colder over the years, and I love nothing more than a good old game of cat and mouse.

"Seems like Joey's lost for words," I say, looking to Bray. His eyes are still fixed on Joey, his gun still trained on him. I move beside Bray and place my hand on top of his, pushing down gently to indicate that the gun isn't needed. He gives me a quizzical look, but Bray would never question me. He's a good boy, does as he's told, never asks for a reason.

I can feel Tony watching our exchange out of the corner of his eye. I turn my head towards him and give him a nod. He hesitates for a second before lowering the gun, clicking the safety on and putting it back into the waistband of his trousers.

"I get the feeling that the conversation that Mr Valentine and I need to have can't be done in the presence of others. Bray, Tony, wait here," I instruct.

"Yes, boss," they answer in unison.

"Mr Valentine, follow me," I say before I turn and make my way down the hall. A few steps along I turn back to see that Joey hasn't moved an inch. It pisses me off. He's in my house, my territory, the least he can do is fucking respect me.

"I don't ask twice, Mr Valentine," I say, my tone cold and hard, my eyes narrowing to slits.

Seconds tick by before Joey seems to realise that I meant what I fucking said. He eyes Bray and Tony before stomping in my direction. I turn and continue down the hallway, leading him to my private meeting room. No one is allowed in here except for me and whatever asshole I may be sweet talking. It's a place of business, a place of negotiation, and most importantly, a place where there are no clues as to how I operate my business.

When I reach the door I push it open and wait beside it as Joey follows me inside. Closing the door behind us, I reach for the light which illuminates the room. A mahogany table sits in the middle, eight chairs placed around it, a bookshelf runs all along the left wall, a fire place on the right, and floor to ceiling windows line the back wall which looks out onto the pool house.

"You got eyes on me in here?" Joey asks.

"I've got eyes everywhere, Joey," I say as I stare him down.

There are a couple of cameras in here, but I am the only one that has access to them. I've never needed to be monitored in here. People that come to my house are usually ones that I have done several business deals with, and they are ones that know better than to try and take me down.

I would never just invite random people into my home. The world is a dangerous place, and this is my fortress from the madness that goes on, day in and day out.

"Those eyes of yours are going to be your downfall," he says, his voice low.

"I think you're mistaken, Joey. My eyes are what keeps my ass from hitting the fucking floor."

"You sure about that?" he says as he takes a step towards me. I don't move, I have no reason to. Joey doesn't scare me, but he does make my heart beat wildly. I'm not sure which is worse.

"Why have you come here, Joey?" I ask, the need to know what his game is thrumming through me.

He smirks, and it sends a shiver down my spine. Bugger. The last thing I want to do is give Joey any indication that he can still make my body zing.

He takes another step forward. And another, until he is stood right in front of me, an inch away from touching me. In another life we could have had it all. Our love story could have been great, amazing, soul consuming. But he ended it. He cast me aside, and for that I can never forgive.

"You want to get straight down to business?" he asks, his eyes holding mine.

"Yes."

"Who was the guy, Paige?"

His question throws me for a second, because I have no clue what the hell he is talking about.

"You're going to have to be more specific," I answer, folding my arms across my chest. I am aware that it pushes my breasts up a little, and Joey falters slightly, letting his eyes drift down for a second before they return to holding my gaze.

"Don't play games with me," he says, his voice low, dangerous and fucking delicious.

"I thought that was what we were doing here, playing games, having some fun before I pull your throne from under you."

Joey lets out a laugh before putting his hands either side of my head, palms against the wall, caging me in, forcing me to lean back a little, making me struggle to find my next breath. Bastard.

He lowers his head, eyes blazing, breath feathering over my face.

"You don't want to fuck with me, Paige. You know what I am capable of," he warns.

"Maybe, but you clearly don't know what *I'm* capable of," I reply as I try to battle against my body that wants to turn to jelly for the Adonis that is millimetres away from me. I don't want to be seen as a weak woman, brought to her knees by a man. I've been there before and promised myself that it would never happen again.

"Oh, baby, I know more than you think," Joey says before closing the gap between us and brushing his lips across mine. It takes me by surprise. Throws me for a loop. Messes with my mind. My heart beat accelerates, my body screams at me to give in and take what I have been missing for so long. I want to, oh boy do I want to, but my mind is that little bit stronger. I don't react, on the outside. Inside, I'm a fucking hot mess.

Joey places his lips beside my ear. "Don't ever try to come for me again, Paige, because next time I won't hold back." His warning rings loud and clear, but it doesn't scare me.

I turn my head so that I am looking straight at him.

"I look forward to it," I whisper as I run my tongue across my bottom lip. Joey watches me, and I know that he still wants me. It's fucking obvious, and a total win. If he wants me, then it may throw him off of whatever plan he has cooked up, making my end goal all the easier to reach.

"I suggest you rethink whatever scheme you have concocted," Joey says, his eyes never leaving my lips. I lick them again, and I swear that I hear him stifle a groan.

"I'm not the pathetic girl that you used to know, Joey, and I have no plans to rethink anything."

He chuckles.

"You always did have a determination running through you, Paige, but now, you're playing Russian roulette with your life."

"Do you think so?" I ask, one eyebrow quirked up.

"You wanna get burned, baby?"

Oh fuck, yes, I do.

"You gonna start the fire?" I ask, enjoying every single second of our dangerous flirtation.

"I'm going to light it up under you before you even realise what is happening," Joey replies.

"Once again, I look forward to it, and when I bring you to your knees begging, don't forget that it was me that made it happen. Me that rocked your world. Just me. Only me."

His eyes harden, and he pushes his body against mine, chest to chest.

"You're the only one that's ever rocked my world, Paige, and you damn well know it."

Fuck.

"Then you'll be counting down the days until it happens again," I whisper, my voice losing its edge ever so slightly.

Joey pushes himself back, his hands moving back by his sides. The loss of his closeness has me feeling things that I blocked out years ago. Disappointment being the biggest one.

"Don't ever send another man to try and infiltrate my world, because the next time I have to come here, it won't be ending this amicably."

What the fuck is he talking about?

I don't get a chance to ask him because he's opening the door and walking out, his shoes echoing along the hallway as he goes. I move to look outside of the door, watching his retreating back.

Well, his little visit sure throws up more questions, the first one being, who the hell is the guy that he was talking about? The second being, why the fuck does he still get to elicit a reaction from my body? The third, and possibly the most dangerous is, why do I still feel like I could fall back into his arms and forget all of the hurt and the pain? And that question alone is the one that I refuse to answer, because if I do, then there is no coming back from it.

Chapter Fourteen
Joey

Fuck.

This is not good.

Paige goddamn Roderick is messing with my mind.

Had I just spoken to anyone else about trying to find shit out about my dealings, they would have been dead. No questions asked. But Paige? She's a weakness in my armour. She's disabling my default settings, and that is a danger to my whole existence.

I have built a wall around me, a force field, and a fucking cage that no one can unlock. Except her. She has the key, and I don't even want her to give it back.

I push my foot down on the accelerator as I tear through the night. The dark, empty streets allowing me to clear my mind. Or try to at least.

I let out a growl of frustration as I picture her caged between my arms, my body pushing against hers. I don't feel. I trained myself to block out anything that remotely resembled lust, want, or love. I gave it up years ago, never let myself open back up. But then I didn't expect Paige to come stomping into my world and rock me to my very core all over again.

If anyone were to find out about my feelings surfacing for her, they would deem me a pussy. They would challenge me, call me out, and go after the very thing that has always had my heart. I wouldn't allow it all those years ago, and I certainly won't allow it now.

Paige thinks that she is going to dethrone me. Paige thinks that she is going to be the top dog of this world, and I am the one to blame. I broke her, I can see it in her eyes no matter how much she tries to mask it. I made her push herself, come back fighting, and return stronger than before.

I should be grateful that she's no pushover, that she can hold her own and take men down that dare to challenge her, but the problem is that I want to take her down, only not in the way that she thinks. I'm playing her game for now, but all I really want is for her to be mine. Always have and always will.

She's determined to try and win, but I see the want within her. She still lusts for me, as I do for her. It's not just about a power struggle in the underworld, it's a power struggle of our hearts. And the heart is the most fragile part of our dark souls.

I already know that my threats about taking Paige down are bullshit. I wouldn't ever hurt her. I couldn't. She's stubborn as hell and drives me insane, but that's all part of the chase. A chase I desperately want to win.

My father always told me that you could never bring the one that you loved into this world. He knew. His love was killed. My mother taken from him by his biggest rival. He never recovered, but he threw all of his energy into becoming a nastier bastard, day by day. He took out his rival, but it wasn't enough justice. My father, the great Donald Valentine, died of a broken heart. He never admitted it to anyone but me, and he is the reason that I gave Paige up. If anything had ever happened to her because of me, I never would have come back from that.

And now she's in my fucking world anyway, but on her own merit. She didn't ask anyone for anything. Did it all herself, and I fucking wish that she hadn't.

I was ready to get out of here, leave it all behind, was nearly there, just had the last part of the puzzle to slot into place. And then she showed up, changing the game altogether.

I slam on the brakes at a red light and take a few deep breaths.

Paige changed the game, and I have to play no matter what.

The light turns green and I speed down the road.

I already know that I will spend most of the night driving to calm myself down. Maybe I should just fuck Paige, get her off of my mind, out of my system. I laugh at my ridiculous thought. Fucking her would only intensify what I feel for her. It wouldn't do a damn thing except consume me. Her body on mine, her moans, her soft skin, her dazzling eyes, her lips.

The memory of us before, to what we would be like now blows my mind. It was great between us back then, but we've had years of build-up. Years of missing one another, years of being mad at one another, years of sacrifice. If we were to ever give in to our feelings, I have no doubt it would be explosive, in more ways than one.

Chapter Fifteen
Paige

"What the hell happened?" I shout as I storm through my house, following the blood line that started at the front door and is trailing down the hallway.

Tony is stood by the front door, his face pale, his jaw clenched. Rome is on the floor, hovering over Miles, his hands holding a cloth to the blood seeping out of his side.

Miles is sweating, his skin white, his eyes wide with fear.

"They came out of nowhere, boss," Rome says, his focus never leaving Miles.

"Who did?" I demand. "Who the fuck came onto my property and caused chaos?"

"The Morgan brothers," Tony answers, his tone flat.

"Where's Donovan?" I ask, the anger building inside of me.

"In the back office, looking at the CCTV," Tony replies.

"Jesus fucking Christ," I say with exasperation. "Did you call Dudley?" Dudley is my private doctor, gets paid handsomely to keep his mouth shut and clean up whatever messes that come along.

"He'll be here in five minutes," Tony says.

"I don't think he's gonna make it that long," Rome says, a slight air of panic in his tone.

"Well push fucking harder and make sure he doesn't die," I say, nodding to Miles whose eyes are slowly closing. "And make sure he doesn't black out. We need him alive." With that, I storm down the hallway to the back office. Not my private one, but the one that all of my boys have access to. I want answers, and I want them now.

I storm through the office door, slamming it shut behind me. Donovan doesn't even flinch, doesn't even take his eyes off the computer screen in front of him.

"You found anything?" I ask as I throw my bag down on the floor and go to look at the computer screen myself.

"Not yet," Donovan answers.

"Where the fuck were you?" I question.

"Taking a piss," Donovan replies.

"It's your fucking job to monitor what goes on around here. You should have been more aware."

"Oh, so I can't even take a slash now?"

"Don't fucking answer me back," I yell. "If you taking a piss means that one of my men are down, then you sure as shit better hold the fuck on."

"I can't see into the goddamn future, Paige." Donovan is just as pissed off as I am it seems. The difference here is that I pay the fucker's wages, so if I say that he needs to hold his damn piss, then he better do just that.

My eyes are glued to the screen. I need the cameras to confirm it was the Morgan brothers. I don't doubt Tony's word, but I always make sure that I have concrete proof before I act. Just acting on a whim, or on someone's say so, can get you killed, and I take no chances.

A knock at the door has my eyes whipping from the screen to see who dares to interrupt.

"Who is it?" I bellow.

The door creaks open and Tony pokes his head round. He looks grim.

"Doctor's here, boss," he informs me.

"Good. Get him anything he needs, and I mean anything. Don't interrupt again unless it is to tell me that Miles is dead," I say sharply.

"Understood, boss," Tony says as he closes the door quietly once his head has disappeared.

My eyes return to the computer screen and strike fucking gold. I watch as a car pulls up outside the front of my property. Two men exit, one being Bobby, the other Clive. There is still someone in the driver seat, but it isn't Larry, and I swear to God I'm going to find out who the fuck it is.

Bobby and Clive walk straight onto my property, seeing as someone has left the fucking gates wide open. Whoever was responsible for that is going to be getting a serious lesson in doing their job correctly. Either that or they will end up losing their life. Either way doesn't bother me. People make mistakes, people need to learn. Simple.

I watch as they stalk towards the front door, calmly, in no rush at all. They wait either side of the door, Bobby hiding behind one of the large flower pots that sit beside the front entrance. Clive is hiding to the side of the porch, his back against the wall.

Minutes tick by. The car hasn't moved from the road and Bobby and Clive are looking at the watches on their wrist. Clive's lips move as he seems to be counting down.

Not two minutes later and the front door opens, Miles walking out. Clive and Bobby abandon their clock watching and take their weapons of choice out of the back of their trousers. Bobby a gun, Clive a knife. It all happens quickly, but I'll be watching it back in slow motion many times in the next hour or so. Bobby springs up from behind the flower pot, surprising Miles who clearly loses his ability to detect any fucking danger as he whirls around to look at Bobby, giving Clive the perfect opportunity to come at him from behind.

Clive pushes the knife into Miles side, Miles collapses, and Bobby and Clive flee the scene, jumping back into the car and driving away.

It's that simple. No high end operation, no clever tactics to try and outsmart my guys. It's all so fucking simple. Too simple. And I have one question on my mind that will need answering within the next few minutes.

Where the fuck is Trevor? He guards the gates, oversees any trouble being moved swiftly along. With no sign of him, he better hope that he's already dead because as far as I'm concerned, he's already signed his own death warrant.

Chapter Sixteen
Paige

I've been pacing the floor for the last half an hour, waiting for Trevor. I watched the cameras, played them back several times. Seems Trevor opened the gates just before the Morgan brothers showed up. There was no reason for him to open them, unless of course he is in cahoots with the brothers. I know what I believe.

Miles is still being monitored by doctor Dudley. It was touch and go several times, but Miles has remained stable for the last hour. Doctor Dudley will monitor Miles until I deem it unnecessary. He's on my books and he knows better than to argue with me.

I hear the front door open and then close, and I know that Donovan just walked in here with Trevor. Trevor, as far as I know, remains unaware that Miles nearly died. No one has said anything to him, and Donovan won't have given Trevor any warning of what is to come.

I crack my knuckles, shake my head from side to side and walk towards the front door. I'm dressed in a pair of jogging bottoms, a tight black T-shirt, and a pair of trainers. I want to be comfortable for what I am about to do. It's not my usual attire, but it's my outfit of choice for ridding the world of one more asshole.

I walk calmly whilst inside of me is like a furnace waiting to explode. Bray and Tony are standing by the front door, their expressions neutral. I know they want to get their hands on Trevor just as much as I do. Rule number one, never shit on your own doorstep. Trevor obviously thought he was above this rule. Fucking fool.

"Don, Trevor," I say with a nod of my head. Donovan nods back.

"Boss," Trevor says, looking completely unprepared for what lies ahead.

"I want to show you both something," I say, turning around and making my way to the meeting room where I was with Joey not even twenty-four hours ago. I don't usually bring my boys in here to give them a dressing down, but today I will make an exception, because Trevor isn't going to be able to read what is coming next.

I hear Donovan and Trevor's foot steps behind me. I enter the meeting room and stand by the door, waiting for them to walk in. When they do, I shut the door and turn to face them. Donovan knows what my plans are. He is fully prepared for what is about to happen.

I don't even have to tell him to come and stand next to me, leaving Trevor stood on his own.

"Trevor," I start, my voice even. "How's things been around here today?"

"All good, boss. Nothing to report," he says, standing tall, his hands clasped behind his back.

"You sure about that?" I question.

"I haven't been made aware of anything that needs reporting," he replies, and I see him gulp, the Adam's apple in his throat bobbing.

"I see," I say as I take a step forward. "So, tell me, why did you open the gates earlier today?"

"The gates?"

"Yes, Trevor, the gates, the great big fucking gates that lead onto my property," I say, losing my cool slightly.

"I opened them for you, when you left this morning."

"I am fully aware of that, Trevor, but why did you open them at twelve thirty-five?"

I see the moment he realises what I already know. I see the panic flash across his face, and I relish in the fact that he is a few short minutes away from squirming and begging for his life.

"I... I..." His stuttering shows his guilt. He clearly didn't think through how he was going to get away with this.

"You know, Trevor, you've worked for me for the last two years. I thought you knew better than to betray me," I say, each word spoken slowly so he doesn't miss the fucking point.

"I thought that you had respect for me, and for where I came from, and for where I have gotten to. What I didn't expect was for you to go behind my back and bring violence to my doorstep."

I expect violence in the world I live in, but not on my property. Not at my private residence, and certainly not brought to me by one of my own.

"I swear, I didn't—"

"Don't lie to me, Trevor," I say, cutting him off. "Don't even waste your breath, because all it will do is piss me off further."

Trevor has the decency to clamp his mouth shut at this point.

I only have one question to ask, because I wouldn't trust anything else that came out of his mouth right now.

"Why, Trevor? Why the fuck would you give the Morgan brothers an opening to come after one of us?"

The question hangs in the air, Trevor knowing his time is running out. He's seen me in action. He's been part of the action, and now he's going to be on the receiving end.

"They took Grace," he answers, his head going down.

Grace is his wife, his pregnant wife. They've been together since they were sixteen, been together for twenty years, and now the Morgans have her.

"They sent me photos of her, tied to a chair, blindfolded, gagged. They asked me to open the gates. I had no idea what their plans were, but they said if I didn't open them then they would cut the baby out of her. I couldn't take the risk, I couldn't just—"

I hold my hand up to silence him. I've dealt with my fair share of assholes, but this is a whole new level.

"Why didn't you just come and tell me?" I say.

"They said that if I told anyone then they would torture her, record it, force me to watch it before they killed them both," he says, tears forming in his eyes with each and every word.

"And you doubted that I could stop that from happening?" I ask.

"I didn't doubt you, boss, I just couldn't take the risk," he admits looking defeated. I take a second, watching his six foot frame bent over, his face showing the pain that he is feeling, and his dark brown eyes looking lifeless, the hope slowly seeping out of them.

No matter what he is going through, I can't help myself, and I walk up to him and punch him on his jaw. I hear my knuckles connect and his head snaps to the side. He won't retaliate, he knows better than that.

"You fucking idiot," I say, teeth gritted as I try to reign in my anger at the situation that we have found ourselves in. I was ready to end Trevor, make him pay for betraying me, but with the news about Grace coming to light, I don't think I can bring myself to do it to him, or to her.

"I'm sorry, boss," Trevor says weakly.

"I don't want your apologies, they mean nothing. What I want is for my fucking boys to stop hiding shit from me and bring me into the goddamn loop!" First Miles and now Trevor. Granted, Miles's behaviour was his own doing, but Trevor? Trevor simply did what he thought was right at the time to keep his family alive.

Trevor doesn't say another word, and Donovan stays silent behind me.

"Where is Grace now?" I ask, needing to know that she is safe. Grace may be Trevor's wife, but she's also my friend. I know that I don't let people close, but Grace has always been pleasant, friendly and has told me that she considers me part of her family. Grace has always known the stakes of Trevor working for me, she has always known that one day it could be his last, but fuck, I thought he had betrayed me and then she would have been left alone. With a baby. Motherfuck.

"The Morgan brothers still have her," Trevor answers. "They won't let her go yet. I presume they are waiting to make sure that there are going to be no repercussions of their attack earlier."

"Fuck," I say out loud. "Do you know where they are keeping her?"

Trevor shrugs, shaking his head. He must feel fucking useless.

"Where do they take their victims, Don?" I ask, keeping my eyes on Trevor and my back to Donovan.

"We don't know," Donovan answers.

I whirl around at his reply. "We don't fucking know?"

Donovan nods and I feel like my control has slipped a little. I pride myself on knowing the ins and outs of everyone that I have had, or have, dealings with. The Morgan brothers slipped beneath my radar, and after our chat earlier this week, I should have done more digging. I presumed that my visit to them would have been enough to send a clear message to them about not fucking with me, or my boys. I guess they didn't get the memo.

"Well, go and do some digging, find out everything that you can. We need to get Grace back," I tell Donovan.

"On it," Donovan answers and then exits the room.

I turn back to Trevor. "What you did was fucking stupid, but we're going to get Grace back," I tell him.

His eyes glaze over as he looks at me with desperation.

"Thank you, boss," he says.

"Don't thank me yet, thank me when she's home safe, and never, ever, go behind my back again. Do I make myself clear?" I say with authority.

"Yes, boss."

"Good. Now, go and splash some water on your face and then get your ass back in here. We're not leaving this room until we find out where they are."

Chapter Seventeen
Joey

"You have a visitor, Joey," Raymond announces as he walks into my office.

"Oh? And who might that be?" I respond, wondering why I have been interrupted when I told my men that I didn't want to be bothered whilst I was in here. I'm at Club Valentine and have a shit load of paperwork to sort through, and interruptions just delay the mind-numbing boredom of making sure that my extra-curricular activity money is hidden.

Before Raymond can respond a voice calls out.

"It's me."

I look up and see Paige round the door as she waltzes into my office. She has a determined look on her face, and is looking far from her usual glam, boss bitch self. She stands there in jogging bottoms, a black, fitted T-shirt and trainers. Her hair is pulled back into a ponytail, her face is free from any make-up, and she has never looked more beautiful.

Raymond raises one eyebrow at me and I dismiss him with a wave of my hand. As he heads to the door, he looks at me inquisitively, and I know that he will want to know why Paige is walking in here and just saying the words, "It's me."

It's not how I conduct business. It's too familiar, and it throws up questions.

The door clicks shut, and I lean back in my chair, drinking in every bit of Paige that I can. Since waltzing back into my life, she has always been in business mode. Never allowing a glimpse of another side of her. Yet now, in this moment, she is showing me another side. She is showing me that whatever she has come here for is of more importance than her portrayal of being the leading boss bitch, and she looks slightly vulnerable.

"What can I do for you, Paige?" I ask, wanting to know the reason for her abrupt visit.

She grinds her teeth together, and I know that she really doesn't want to ask me for anything. I smirk. It's quite a turnaround from her behaviour earlier.

"I need to ask for your help," she says so quietly that the thumping music in the background almost masks her words. Almost.

"My help?" I question, knowing that her saying those words must be killing her. "Take a seat." I gesture to the chair opposite me, on the other side of my desk. She walks forward and sits, her back straight, one leg crossed over the other and her hands linked around her knee.

"I need some information," she starts. "One of my boys was stabbed earlier on today, and another has had his wife taken from him. His pregnant wife. I need to find her."

Well, I hadn't expected that to come out of her mouth.

"What information are you hoping to find answers to?" I ask.

"I need to know where the Morgan brothers take their victims when they want to keep them hidden away," she says, more forthcoming than I thought that she would be this early on in the conversation. I thought that I would have to coax answers out of her, but she's giving them up freely, and that indicates that she has exhausted all of her usual avenues of finding out intel.

"And how exactly are the Morgan brothers involved?" I ask, needing to know exactly what I may be getting myself into, because let's face it, I'm going to fucking help Paige no matter what, I just need to be prepared for a fallout on my end.

"Because they're assholes who have a grudge against my boy that got stabbed."

"And why do they have a grudge?"

"Because he fucked their sister." She stares at me, her mouth set in a straight line.

"And they found out?"

"Yes. I met with them, redrew the battle lines and they fucking ignored me. I've had a deal with them for years, and they just broke the fragile bond that we shared."

Paige is beyond pissed, and rightly so. I would be baying for their blood if I were in her shoes.

"So why not just go and finish them?" I ask.

"Because I need my boy's wife back first. I can't allow them to hurt her, or keep her," she says, showing me a little of the compassion that I always loved about her.

Loved? Get your head out of your ass, Valentine. Love destroys people, so keep your head out of the fucking clouds.

"Your boy that was stabbed, is he alive?"

"He's hanging in there," she informs me.

"And the wife is how pregnant?"

"Seven months."

Fucking hell. The Morgan brothers have really gone and signed their own death certificate. Fucking with Paige is one thing, but with a pregnant woman who is involved in her clan? She's going to rip them apart with her bare hands, I can see the want to do so on her beautiful face. Makes my dick want to come to life if I'm honest. Her fierce nature is like a fucking aphrodisiac.

"I presume she is still alive?" I have to ask the question.

"As far as we are aware. The Morgan brothers are waiting to see if I come for them in the wake of the attack on my boy before they give her back." Her eyes blaze with pent up anger, and I know that I am going to enjoy seeing her in action.

"Anything else I need to know?"

"I don't think so."

"And what do I get for giving you this information?" I ask, because the whole point of helping someone out is to get a return yourself, but at this point I'm just curious to see what Paige has to say. I don't expect anything from her but her respect. That would be enough for me.

"Whatever you want," she says, shocking the shit out of me.

Silence stretches between us and I know that this woman that the Morgan brothers have taken is more important than just being one of her boys' wives. She likes this woman and has forged some sort of bond with her. Paige wouldn't just give away anything unless you were part of what she deems her family.

"I want your respect," I say honestly.

"You already have it," she replies, her tone never wavering. Well, I wasn't expecting that answer. She sure seems intent on surprising the hell out of me tonight.

"You've got a funny way of showing it, Paige."

"Well I'm telling you that I do respect you, but I'm not about to get down on my knees and kiss your fucking shoes to prove it," she says, and I can't help the laughter that leaves my mouth.

"And everything that has happened up to now clearly shows your respect for me, and for what I do," I respond sarcastically.

"Oh please, Joey, everything up to now has been banter. Don't participate if you can't handle the comebacks."

Oh, she is full of fucking sass, and I'm going to enjoy every last minute of what is to come next.

"Banter, huh?" Two of the most powerful people in the underworld, and she's putting our previous conversations down to banter.

"I didn't come here for you to gloat, but I get that this must be satisfying for you. Me asking for help, you having the power," she says, and she isn't fucking wrong. I am thrilled that she has come to me, but not for the reasons that she is thinking. It's more about the fact that she came to me at all, even with everything that went down between us years ago.

"You've got me all wrong, Paige."

"Oh yeah? How?" she asks, cocking her head to the side.

I lean forward, bracing my elbows on my desk. "This has never been about a power struggle for me. I get that you want to take me down. I get that you want your name to reign supreme in this fucked up world we live in, but I don't give a damn about being the top dog. I give a damn about making things right, with this world, with the way shit goes down, and with us."

I don't miss the intake of her breath at my words. She puts on a good front, I'll give her that, but she isn't fooling me.

"There is no 'us,' Joey."

"Oh, baby, you know damn well that there is." I call her bluff, expect her to keep her defences up, but she shocks me once again.

"You hurt me, Joey. You threw me away like a piece of trash. You made me feel worthless, and I promised myself that no one would ever make me feel like that again." Her honesty echoes around the walls.

"Is that why you came into this world? To prove something to me?" I ask.

"No. I came into this world to prove to myself that I was worth more." She holds her head high, and fuck if her words don't do things to me. The tension simmers between us. The air becoming hotter. I'm not a mushy guy. I don't do romance, don't do feelings, or at least I haven't since Paige. And with her here, opening up a little bit more to me, I want nothing more than to take her in my arms and show her how fucking sorry I am, but I know that she doesn't need that right now. She needs my help, and she's got it.

"Do you have a plan in place for when you find out where the Morgan brothers have hidden her?" I ask, changing the subject before shit gets awkward between us.

"Oh yeah, I have a plan," she says, her eyes lighting up.

"You better tell me what the plan is before we go in there and get your girl back."

"We?" she asks, eyebrows raised.

"Yes, Paige. We."

"I only came here for information, not for you to do anything else," she says adamantly.

"And I won't get involved without being there beside you."

Now it's her turn to look shell-shocked.

"I have no intention of trying to take over. Anything that happens to those brothers is your call. I'm just there to reiterate the message of staying the fuck away," I tell her.

"The message won't need reiterating because they won't live to see another day once I'm finished with them," she informs me, and damn if her words don't set my insides alight.

"I'm all ears," I say holding my hands out either side of me.

Paige grins wickedly, and I know that what she is about to tell me is going to be one of the most savage revenge plans ever made. A woman burned, never underestimate them.

Chapter Eighteen

Paige

I left Joey's club to return to my house. Once there, I filled Donovan and the rest of the boys in on what was going to happen now. Donovan was the only one that knew that I was going to see Joey, so the rest of them were pretty shocked, but they soon got over it when I told them what was in store for the Morgan brothers. I have never done a collaboration with anyone before, so this is new territory for me.

After speaking with my boys, I went and changed my clothes, opting for my usual business attire so that I was dressed ready to kill, literally. From my black trouser suit to the cream coloured blouse beneath the fitted jacket, from the killer stilettos to the sleek ponytail, from the red lipstick to the smoky eye effect, I know that I look every inch the boss that I am. I also know that beneath all of this there is a monster inside waiting to be unleashed on the bastards that invaded my world.

My boys have their instructions, and I'm sat in a car with Joey. His car. Just the two of us.

Four of my boys are following, as are six of Joey's. Both of our private homes are guarded, ready for an attack that may come off of the back of what we are about to do.

Joey remains adamant that all he wants is my respect. I'm dubious. This is Joey fucking Valentine we're talking about. He doesn't do something for nothing, but right now, he's about to go and bust some balls with me, so I can't really complain about him having the upper hand. My actions tonight have cemented him firmly at the top of the chain. My mission to take him down is on hold, maybe permanently.

He's dressed in dark denim jeans that fit him like a glove, a tight, black tank top and a black shirt that he has left open. What I wouldn't give to tear that shirt off and lift the tank top, exposing the abs that I know are there. Joey is a man who takes care of himself, prides himself on his appearance and the way that he handles his business. A man after my own heart.

Fuck. I need to stop thinking about him like that. I don't need any distractions. I can't afford to lower my guard, ever, and I want revenge on the Morgan brothers more than I want revenge on Joey.

"You okay?" Joey asks, dragging me from my own thoughts.

I turn to look at him and his ice blue eyes that still get my panties in a twist. Fuck.

"I'm good," I reply before turning back to looking out of the car window.

"We're five minutes away," he informs me. I just nod my head, not sure if he is looking at me or not.

My mind seems intent on reminding me of the Joey that I used to know. As we move along the road, the image of Joey and I being close, being in love and being ultimate fucking couple goals enters my head.

"You know what I love the most about you, Paige?" Joey says as he places kisses along my jaw line, stopping when he reaches my mouth, hovering above my lips to deliciously torture me.

"My peachy ass?" I reply with a cheeky smile.

Joey moves his hand and places it on said ass before he squeezes it gently, sinking his fingers into my flesh slowly.

"Nothing better than this ass," he says, and I giggle. I love how he makes me feel. Empowered, sexy, loved. I've never met anyone like him. "But no, that's not it."

"Hmmm, how about my wicked sense of humour?" I say, wiggling my eyebrows.

"Wrong again."

"My eyes?"

"They are beautiful, but that's still not the correct answer," he says, smiling.

"You gonna keep making me guess, Joey? Or are you just going to tell me and then show me again how I'm all yours?" I say, my voice ending on a whisper. Joey claiming me, making me his has been the best thing to ever happen to me.

His hand moves from my ass, his fingers trailing up my side until they reach my face. He brushes a strand of hair off of my cheek, tenderly, softly, lovingly.

The smile disappears from his face and his eyes look into my intensely.

"The thing I love most about you, Paige, is your heart."

"My heart?"

"Yeah, baby, your heart. I've never met anyone like you, Paige. You are beautiful inside and out, but that heart of yours is bigger than anything else. It let me in. You let me in, and you let me love you. You accept me for who I am. You don't try to change me or mould me into someone else."

His words have the heart that he is talking about pumping a little bit faster.

"Not only did you let me in, but you gave me your love back. My world meant nothing before you, Paige. I don't ever want to let go of what we have."

"You won't have to," I whisper, tears pooling in my eyes from his honesty.

"I worry that one day I might have to."

"Why?"

"I can't explain why, it's just a fear that I have," he says *and my heart melts on the fucking spot. Joey Valentine, scared of losing me? Never going to happen.*

"Joey, I'm not going anywhere," I tell him, meaning *every fucking word.*

"You can't say that, Paige."

"Yes, I can, and I'm telling you that we are so much stronger together than we are apart. We fit, Joey. Me and you, us against the world, big guy."

"Paige."

"Hmmm?"

"We're here," Joey says as he stops the car. I shake the memories from my head and take a good look at our surroundings.

We're parked down a side road, Cotswold stone walls that are four foot high on the right, and a large field on the left with what looks like a derelict barn in the middle of it.

"The Morgan brothers will have Grace in that barn over there," Joey tells me as he nods to the left.

"What's behind the wall?" I ask.

"The house that they all run to when they act like the little bitches that they are," Joey tells me.

"How long have they had this place?"

"Just over five years."

"And no one else knows about it?"

"No."

"So how did you find it?" I ask, and I know that the question is a fucking stupid one the moment that it has left my mouth.

"Paige, I make it my business to know everything," Joey says.

"You didn't know about me," I reply with a smirk.

"You're the exception."

"Bet you hated not knowing who Miss Roderick was," I reply, my smile widening.

Joey laughs, and I know that he doesn't have a comeback for that. He would have been pissed that he couldn't get close enough to unmask me before I revealed myself to the underworld.

A car pulls up behind us and I know that it is Joey's men. My guys are set up on the other side of the Morgan's property, and more of Joey's will be scouring the field for a possible threat. All we're waiting for is a signal from his right hand man, Raymond, to let us know that we can forge ahead with our part of the plan.

Joey already knows that the Morgan brothers have no surveillance here. Fucking stupid move on their part, but I guess they think that they are safe, seeing as they have been here undetected for five years. Until now.

Joey's phone rings and he pulls it out of his pocket, answers it and puts it to his ear.

"We good, Ray?" he says, and I stay silent as Raymond relays the relevant information to him.

"Good... No, stay put... We're going in." He ends the call and turns to me. "You ready?"

I feel a wicked smile tug at my lips.

"More than ready."

Chapter Nineteen
Joey

Paige gets out of the car, shutting the door quietly and I do the same. She rounds the car and stands beside me, where she always should have been.

"I'll follow," I tell her. She nods and starts to move towards the wall that surrounds the house. I have my gun in my hand already, always prepared, never letting anyone get the upper hand. Except for maybe Paige, but I can't think about that right now. I have work to do, and this is going to be the first time that I see Paige in action. Is it weird that it does something to me to know that she can handle the gun that is in her hand? Is it weird that I can't wait to see her kick some ass all over the place? Weird or not, it's a fucking turn on to see her strutting her stuff in those come-fuck-me heels.

Damn.

I follow her as she makes her way to the gate at the front of the property. She scours the area, her eyes sweeping the grounds to make sure that we haven't alerted the bastards that sit inside the country house that has seen better days.

I'm more than shocked that the Morgans have left themselves wide open with nothing here to act as a deterrent to unwanted company. Fucking morons. They are the worst kind of wannabe gangsters. Hot tempered, quick to jump in with their fists and fuck all common sense to know that their time in this game is coming to an end.

I won't be sorry to see them get their comeuppance. They have pissed off plenty of people over the years, but they always managed to either talk their way out of it, or they put an end to the fuckers that wanted to take them out. This time though they won't get a chance to end the woman coming after them. Paige knows what she is doing, and I have her back. They won't be getting out of this alive.

Paige moves onto the property, slipping through the half-open gate. I follow, my eyes trained on anything and everything. I have been built for this, to hunt, to keep myself safe, to rid the world of a few more assholes.

We move across the driveway, our feet moving quickly but quietly. I'm astounded that Paige can move so swiftly in those heels. Heels that would feel fucking great wrapped around the back of my neck whilst my tongue is buried inside of her.

Paige moves to the front door, stopping on the left whilst I take up residence on the right. She looks at me and gives a nod of her head before she moves in front of the door and kicks the fucker open. One kick is all it takes for the door to swing and bang into the wall behind it.

"What the hell?" I hear shouted from inside.

Paige smirks and just stands there, waiting for the Morgan's to come and greet her. I stay hidden for the time being. My entrance will come in the next few minutes.

"What the fuck are you doing here?" I hear one of them say, pretty sure that it's Larry.

"Good evening, boys," Paige says in a sickly sweet voice. "I do hope that I'm not interrupting anything?"

"Damn fucking right you're interrupting," Clive shouts back. His voice is more distinctive than the other two of the brothers.

"Now, now, Clive, no need to be so hostile," Paige says, a smile on her face. "And no need to point the gun at me. I'm just here for a friendly chat."

"Friendly chat my ass," Larry says.

"Why are you here? And how the fuck did you find us?" Clive asks.

"So many questions and not even an offer of a cup of tea," Paige answers. She's playing with them, cat and mouse.

"Don't try and be fucking cute, Paige," Larry says.

"Cute? You're calling me cute?" Paige laughs wickedly. "Oh, Larry, you should know by now that I am anything but cute."

"Give me one good reason why I shouldn't put a bullet in your head right fucking now," Larry shouts and this is my cue to come out of the shadows.

I step up behind Paige and take in the look of shock on Larry and Clive's faces.

"I don't think that would be a very good idea," I say, and I wish I had a fucking camera so that I could look back and laugh at their expressions.

"Joey Valentine," Larry says. "What are *you* doing here, and with *her*?" he says, his distaste for Paige showing in his tone.

I move to stand beside her. "You don't get to ask me questions, ever," I say with finality. Larry has the good sense to shut his mouth. "And put the fucking gun down whilst you're keeping your mouth shut."

Larry looks to Clive and I see him gulp. He knows that they are screwed right now. The Morgan brothers made a pact with my father years ago to stay the fuck away from anything related to Valentine business. The fact that my dad took out theirs showed them how serious he was. Of course they tried to exact a revenge plan, but of course it failed, and they were given a choice by my father to either stay away or he was going to make sure that everyone in the underworld would fuck them up so badly that they would wish that they were dead. He tortured them for a few days before they were given a choice, so they were fully aware of what would lie ahead for them.

They chose the first option. I upheld my father's wishes to leave them be. He always said that they would never cross me, and now that I am on their doorstep, they look like rabbits caught in the headlights. I don't kill men just for the sake of it, I only ever do it with a reason, but I'll make an exception for these wankers.

"Shall we start again, boys?" Paige says, and I can hear the smugness in her tone. They both look at her, waiting for her next words. "Good evening, fuckers," she says as she walks into the house. "Follow me." She walks past them and into a room on the left. They both look at me like little lost sheep.

"You heard the lady, get fucking moving," I bark at them. They scurry into the room after Paige and I follow, kicking the front door shut before I do.

When I enter the room that Paige went in, my nose screws up at the acrid smell. My eyes sweep the room and take in the dark green walls, shitty brown floor, and navy blue chairs with various rips in the fabric.

"Sit," Paige tells them both and they do so, against their will. "Where's Bobby?" she asks.

"Not telling," Larry answers. Before anyone can say another word, Paige walks the few feet to him and socks him straight across the cheek.

"Argh," he says as his head flies to the side. I see Clive reach for his gun, but before I can tell him to put it the fuck away, Paige reaches across, one hand going around his throat and the other knocking the gun out of his hand. I wait by the doorway because we still don't know where Bobby is at this moment in time, but I have to admit that Paige exudes nothing but control right now.

"Get off of me, you crazy bitch," Clive splutters. I see Paige tighten her grip on his throat and then her knee is firmly planted between his legs. The roar of pain he lets out is quite satisfying.

Larry looks like he's about to try and have a go, but Paige soon has her gun pointing in his face with her free hand whilst still locking her fingers around Clive's throat.

"Don't be fucking stupid, Larry," she warns him, her tone ice cold.

Larry looks indecisive for a few seconds, but quickly seems to realise that Paige isn't fucking around.

"I asked you a question and I expect you to answer it," she says, her eyes blazing with fury, but I know that this is just the start. This is just Paige getting warmed up. If I were a lesser man, my dick would be hard as rock right now, but luckily for me, I've been in this game for a long time and can control myself.

"He went for a walk," Clive says with a snarl across his face. Paige takes a moment to look at me, and I take that as a cue to intervene.

"Answer the fucking question, Clive, unless you would prefer to have it beaten out of you," I say.

"Pfft, you think that your threat of using me as a punching bag is going to get me to talk? Come on, Joey, you're not new to this, and you know damn well that particular threat isn't going to work," Clive says, trying to act like the big man.

Paige lets out an evil laugh before she punches him in the face. His nose starts to spurt blood everywhere and his howl of pain echoes off of the walls.

Larry looks like he is about to jump out of his seat, so I calmly walk over and place my gun against his head, still making sure I have a view of the door, just in case Bobby makes himself known.

No words are exchanged as Larry gives me a filthy look before training his eyes back on Paige.

"Okay, Clive, you wanna do this the hard way?" Paige says.

"Is there any other way?" he goads her.

She chuckles, and fuck does it make me want to pick her up and take her back to my place, to my bed, to a place she never should have left.

"Oh, Clive," she says with a shake of her head. "I thought that we had come to an agreement when our meeting ended the other day." She tuts a few times before continuing. "Fuck where Bobby is, we'll find him soon enough. You already know why I've come here."

"Miles got what was coming to him," Larry bites out and Clive shoots him a look.

Paige turns her attention to Larry, releasing her grip on Clive's throat and moving back a few steps.

"Do you think so?"

"You bet I fucking do," Larry replies. He's a stupid, stupid man. All he is doing is stoking the beast. I push my gun into his head, nudging him, making him grunt.

"You thought that you could come onto my private property and get away with stabbing one of my boys?" Paige says, and her voice has taken on a new edge. Low, dark and full of danger. *Come on, baby, show me what you got.*

"He deserved it," Larry reiterates.

"All because your sister couldn't keep her loose legs shut," Paige retorts, and that is when all hell breaks loose. Clive lunges at Paige, Larry tries to knock the gun out of my hand but very quickly finds out that was a big mistake. I grab the fucker round the throat and pull him up from his seat, surging forwards, pushing him towards the wall. I pin him in place and squeeze my fingers tighter and tighter. Larry grabs my hand with both of his and tries to pull me off, but he's no match for me. I can see the fight leaving his eyes as he squirms like the fucking worm that he is. His foot connects with my shin, causing me to flinch slightly, but I soon recover and go to work on his face. Punch after punch, the blood flying everywhere.

"You know," I start as I stop punching him for a few to ask him something that I think I already know the answer to. "I do have a question for you, Larry."

"Oh yeah?" he says, spitting some blood from his mouth onto the floor.

"You sent that guy to my office and got him to say that it was Paige, didn't you?"

"What guy?" he says.

"Don't try and be a smart-ass, Larry, just answer the fucking question," I say as I push my arm on his neck, cutting off a little of his air supply.

"If you keep pushing your arm on my neck, then I won't be able to give you a fucking answer." His face is getting paler by the second.

"Then answer faster," I retort.

A few seconds more pass by before he squeals like a pig.

"Yeah, that's right, it was us. That was our way of saying fuck you, Valentine," Larry spits out before I sock him square in his mouth. He drops to the floor like a sack of shit as the blow I landed on him knocks him out cold. I turn around to see Clive knocking Paige on her ass and it lights a fucking ferocity within me that I didn't even know existed. I'm a ruthless bastard at the best of times, but right now I want to kill Clive with my bare hands just for touching her.

I walk the few feet to where they are and grab Clive like a fucking rag doll, tossing him across the room. He lands with a thud on the other side of the room, going limp.

The only sounds left to be heard are those of mine and Paige's deep breaths.

I turn to look at her as she gets up, wiping the corner of her mouth with her hand.

"You okay?" I ask her, seeing that her bottom lip has been split open slightly.

"I'm good," she says, stony-faced.

I pull my phone out of my pocket and call Raymond. He answers before the first ring has even cut off.

"Ray, did you get Grace?" I ask him.

"Yes," he confirms.

"Good. Send Nate and Pascal to round things up here."

"Sure thing, Joey," Raymond replies, and I cut the call.

"Why did you do that?" Paige says, walking towards me with a questioning look on her face.

"Do what? Call Raymond?"

"No. Why did you intervene?"

"Are you serious?"

"Yes, Joey, I am." She stands there, her arms folded across her chest, and looking every inch the fucking woman of my dreams.

I turn my body so that I am completely facing her. I still have my gun in my hand and I click the safety on before placing it in the waistband of my jeans.

"Joey," she says again when I still haven't answered her.

"What do you want me to say, Paige?"

"I want you to answer my question."

"Isn't it obvious why I intervened?" I ask, wondering what it is she wants to hear.

"Not really."

"Oh, come on, Paige, as if I was going to stand here and let him hurt you," I tell her, finding it fucking ridiculous that she is even asking me this question.

"I had it under control."

"I never thought for a second that you didn't, but I saw you fall to the floor and I jumped in on instinct."

"Instinct," she repeats my words. "So, instinct had you fucking up the plan?"

"I think it's fairly obvious that the plan didn't follow what we had discussed from the moment that Clive lunged at you," I tell her.

"I could have handled him, Joey," she says, her eyes narrowing slightly and her voice going lower.

I take a step towards her, unsure of what the fuck I am doing, but whatever it is, I want to carry on.

"I don't see the big deal," I say with a shrug of my shoulders.

"You wouldn't," she replies, exasperated.

"Then enlighten me, Paige," I say, my head tilting to the side and my feet still moving towards her.

"I don't need you to save me, Joey," she says as I get within two steps of her.

"I never said you did." One more step.

"I'm not some damsel in distress, and I'm not yours to save," she says, the determination slipping from her voice.

I'm one step away from her, one step away from ending the tension between us and opening up a whole other can of worms. Is the can of worms worth it? It appears so as I take that last step towards her. We're toe to toe, chest to chest, my hands cupping her face.

"You've always been mine, Paige, but somewhere along the line you forgot," I say before I place my lips on hers and do what I have wanted to do ever since I saw her walk into the party that she threw to reveal herself.

Her hands find my waist and I kiss her harder until our tongues are meeting one another, tasting one another, devouring one another.

Her fingers dig into my hips as her body presses against mine. I tilt her head back a little more and move my hand to the nape of her neck, gripping her gently.

Her fingers slide their way beneath my top and trail over my abs. We're both lost in the moment, lost to each other, when a shout from the front door breaks us from our bubble.

"Boss?" I hear Nate say and Paige and I spring apart at the sudden intrusion. She touches her lips and I hold her gaze for a second before Nate and Pascal walk in and take a look at the Morgan brothers lying on the floor.

"You want them taken to the usual place, boss?" Nate says, and I simply nod at him.

"Keep a look out for Bobby," I tell them. "They wouldn't give up where he was," I say as I look at the two pieces of trash currently being dragged across the floor.

"Sure thing, boss," Nate replies.

Within minutes they have the Morgan brothers removed from the room, leaving me alone with Paige.

"We need to get going," she says as she walks past me and heads for the door. "Oh, and I want to know where the usual place is that you keep the assholes that you need to interrogate. Those brothers are all mine," she says before disappearing from sight.

So, I guess we're back to business then. For now.

Chapter Twenty
Paige

I'm an idiot. A total fucking idiot. Why did I let Joey kiss me? What the hell was I thinking?

The questions roll around my mind as I make my way back to Joey's car. I shouldn't even be getting in the damn car with him, but I stupidly decided to ride with him and not bring my own car. His idea of course, but then I never envisioned that our evening would end up with Clive and Larry still being alive, Bobby nowhere to be fucking found, and Joey and I kissing.

I open the car door, get in and slam the fucker shut. I am beyond pissed off with myself. I let my guard down, let Joey see a vulnerability in me. Motherfucking bollocks.

Joey appears a moment later, walking towards the car, looking every inch the handsome devil that he is.

When he gets in I turn to look out of the window. The quicker this car ride goes, the better. I need to get myself together and get back to being the heartless bitch that I made myself into.

Joey starts the car and reverses down the road. The other guys have all gone. I already know that my boys have got Grace, it was part of the plan. Grace is being taken back to my place, and her and Trevor will stay at mine for as long as it takes for them not to be a target. They wouldn't still be a target had we found out where the fuck Bobby was.

I swear, when I find out where he is, he's going to wish that he had stayed hidden. I know that tonight didn't go quite as planned, but I am going to enjoy torturing the shit out of Larry and Clive.

"Hey," I say as Joey takes a sharp left turn. "What are you doing?"

He's racing down the one track road. If we meet another car then it's going to be our funeral. I'm not scared of a little speed, but I am pissed off that we're not going back to his headquarters.

"Joey, where the fuck are we going?" I say, my voice louder than before. He remains quiet, his jaw tight. When it becomes apparent that he isn't going to divulge anything, I slam my hand against the dashboard and then sit back in my seat, letting out a loud huff. I'm not worried about him hurting me, and even if he wanted to do that, I would give him a good fucking fight. No, what I'm worried about is whether he wants to talk about what just happened.

I don't allow myself to get caught up in ridiculous girly feelings. You get burned bad enough, you don't want to go back for more.

A wall approaches us fast, and Joey shows no signs of slowing down. Maybe he's testing me? Trying to gage how easily I scare? Fucking waste of his time. I won't show weakness. I've already done that by kissing him, so I'll be damned if I'm going to show him another chink in my armour.

The wall gets closer, and I don't see anywhere to turn off. My heartbeat accelerates, my left hand gripping the side of my seat. My right hand remains on my thigh, flat and unquivering. My face is schooled, showing no emotion, but inside I'm wondering when the fuck he's going to slow this car down.

Closer it creeps, less time to stop. I want to scream, I want to shout, I want to grab the damn wheel from him, but I don't. It's Joey Valentine in the driving seat, and he's showing me that he has complete control right now. Fucking bastard.

I breathe a little deeper, grip the seat a little harder, squeeze my legs together ever so slightly, and just when I think that Joey is going to plough us straight into the fucking wall, he brakes, the car lurches, his hand flies to the handbrake, the car skids, turning, and Joey looks completely at ease, but then it's my side of the car that will hit the wall first. I watch, I wait, and within a couple of seconds the car has stopped, ending up lengthways along the wall.

My heart feels like it's going to beat out of my chest. For a moment there I was scared. More scared than standing in a room full of underworld assholes, more scared than having a gun held to my head. I turn to look at Joey and find that the bastard is smiling. Fucking smiling.

"What the hell was that?" I ask before I can stop myself. Joey slowly turns to face me, and I can see the excitement in his eyes. He got a rush out of that shit. He enjoyed every second. Again, bastard.

"That was exhilarating," he replies, still smiling.

"Well, I'm glad you gave yourself a thrill, but what was the point of it?" I can feel my anger building at the fact that he went completely off course just to get some weird high. I get the rush of adrenaline in certain situations but driving a car at a wall just seems fucking stupid.

Joey turns his whole body so he's facing me, his eyes locking with mine.

"You really want to know?" he asks.

"I wouldn't have asked if I didn't," I retort.

"That is how I feel when I'm around you, with you, near you."

"What?" I say, shocked that he is choosing now to try and have a meaningful moment.

"That rush, that fear, the adrenaline pumping wildly, you do that to me, Paige."

"Right," I say, not really sure why he is telling me this. I don't want to listen to his words, but damn do they make me miss the Joey that I used to love. "So, you're telling me that being around me makes you want to drive into a brick wall?"

Joey just looks at me, his jaw clicking. I can't help but screw with him. Sarcasm is my default mode when I'm being forced to deal with shit that I don't want to deal with. I wasn't prepared for this. I never expected for Joey to change the fucking game this dramatically.

"You remember when we first met?" he says, throwing me off once again.

"How could I forget?" I say with the sarcasm that I love so much.

"You need to let go of that fucking rage you hold for me, Paige," Joey says.

"Oh really? You think it's that easy to let go when I've done nothing but hate you ever since you threw me away?" I reply, wishing that I hadn't said any of that. I'm letting him know how much he hurt me, and it's not part of the plan. In fact, none of my plans have worked in regards to Joey, and I went to him for help. Me. Just me. He didn't come knocking on my door. I brought Joey into the loop when I should have kept him at arm's length.

"Hate is a strong word, Paige," Joey comments.

"Yeah? So is love and I gave that up a long time ago." I stare at him, never letting my gaze waver.

"You sure about that?" he questions.

"Positive."

"You don't need to keep fighting me. I'm not your enemy," Joey says, and I really can't be fucking dealing with this right now.

Instead of answering him, I open the car door and get out, slamming it shut before I walk back the way we came.

Being near Joey is bad for me. It wears me down, makes me fucking weak. I won't be weak. I won't be the girl that I once was.

"You can't run away from this, Paige," Joey shouts from behind me. I don't turn around, I don't want to engage in whatever he is trying to do. I need to clear my head, get back to what I do best, and crush the assholes that try to take me down. The trouble is, I don't think I'm going to be able to crush Joey, and I don't even think that I want to. It had been my goal for so long; take him down, reign supreme, but he's flipped everything.

His words, his actions, they speak loudly. How do you get over someone that still has your heart? It pains me to admit it to myself. I focussed on revenge, blocked out the way he used to love me, cherish me and make me feel like I was at the centre of his world.

If you open yourself to another and they let you go, is there really any way of getting over that?

I feel his hand snake around my arm; didn't even hear him coming up behind me.

I whirl around, ripping my arm out of his grasp.

We stand there, staring at one another. Seconds tick by, thoughts swirl around my mind. I remember his touch, his hands, his fingers. He knew how to extract every single emotion from me back then, and as much as I try to hide it now, I fear that he still can.

"What are you running from?" he asks.

What am I running from? From you. From the pain. From the heartache. From the possibility of being crushed all over again.

"Paige," he says quietly, stepping forward and placing his hand on my cheek. I close my eyes for a moment, savouring the feel of the last time that I will let him put his hands on me.

My eyes open, and his ice blues have me wanting to be the weak one. To give in, to allow myself the chance to try again. It would be easier to forgive, would be less confusing, but it would also be the end of everything I am.

"Coming to you for help was a mistake," I say.

His hand drops from my face. His eyes losing some of the hope that I saw there only seconds ago.

I'm strong, I can walk away. And that is exactly what I do as I turn on my heel and put some distance between myself and Joey. This time I don't hear him come for me. I don't even hear the roar of his car engine.

I'm drawing a new line. A line that I won't ever cross again. Joey Valentine makes me a weaker woman, and the power that I have focussed on for so long is still within my grasp. I just need to get my head back in the game, play to win, and forget that I ever went crawling to Joey fucking Valentine.

Chapter Twenty One
Joey

"Donovan just arrived, boss," Raymond says, informing me that Paige's right hand man is here.

"Send him in," I reply, my eyes not moving from my computer screen. A screen that has countless photos of Paige and I together. Happy photos, a simpler time, before the shit hit the fan.

I didn't follow Paige last night. I let her go. She needs time to come to terms with the fact that we still want each other.

"Joey," Donovan says as he enters my office at Club Valentine. I close down the photos on my computer and turn my attention to the man that is closest to Paige. Lucky bastard.

"Donovan, take a seat," I say as I gesture to the chair on the other side of my desk. Donovan walks over and sits down. "What can I do for you?"

"Paige wants to know when you are going to release the Morgan brothers to her," Donovan says. His eyes watch me inquisitively.

"When does she want them?" I ask.

"As soon as possible," he replies.

"And why is Paige sending you to ask her questions?"

"She's busy with business," Donovan says, although I can tell that he isn't convinced by the answer that Paige has so obviously given him.

"The Morgan brothers are her business," I say.

"That's why I'm here, to tie up any loose ends."

To tie up loose ends. Is he sending me a fucking message? Does he know more about my past with Paige than he is letting on?

I survey the way he sits, like he thinks he's got one up on me. He's not scared of dealing with a Valentine, but if he thinks that he has got the upper hand here, he is sadly fucking mistaken.

"Tell Paige to give me a call and I will make the arrangements," I tell him.

"With all due respect, Joey, she sent me to make the arrangements," Donovan says, leaning forward in his chair slightly.

"And I'm telling you that she needs to give me a call." I won't back down on this. He comes in here, thinking he can handle business when he can't handle shit.

"Why? I'm here, we can deal with it now," he replies.

Donovan Marshall. Paige's number one, demanding answers from me. Shit just got a little more messy.

"Donovan, don't forget who you're fucking speaking to," I warn him. "If I tell you that Paige needs to give me a call to make the arrangements, then she needs to give me a fucking call. You don't get to question what I say." I swear, if he thought that he could shoot me in the head and get away with it, he would be doing that right now. Turns out though that Donovan isn't as badass as he tries to make out.

"What is the deal with you and Paige?" he says, and I can instantly see that he knows he shouldn't have said that out loud. Clearly she hasn't told him anything. I don't know whether that's a good or a bad thing. Then again, I haven't told anyone about our history, so I can see why she would want to keep it quiet.

"Have her call me," I say sternly. I don't need to carry on a conversation with him, there's nothing more to say.

He gets up, knowing that he has been dismissed and stalks over to the door. Before he leaves, he turns back around to me.

"Joey, I respect what you do here, I respect who you are, and I respect that you have worked for everything that you have. But if you fuck around with Paige, make no mistake that I will come for you." His words are meant to install some terror inside of me, they do nothing of the sort. But his words do show me that Paige means more to him than being his boss.

"Are you threatening me, Donovan?" I ask, a smirk on my lips.

"Yes." No hesitation, straight forward answer. This fucker is in love with her. You don't put your ass on the line for nothing short of love in this world. He's showing me his weakness, it's just a shame that it's the same fucking weakness as mine.

"Does she know?" I ask the question that I don't need to explain. His jaw tightens, and I know from that movement alone that she doesn't have a clue about Donovan being in love with her.

"You can leave now," I say, dismissing him completely.

Donovan walks away, closes the door behind him, and I sit back in my seat. In the last twenty-four hours I've had more insight into Paige's world than I thought possible.

Donovan is in love with her, I still want her, and Paige is trying to block her feelings. Am I being blind? Does she still want me? That kiss last night tells me that she does, but does she have feelings for Donovan? Is he the reason that she is pushing me away? Or is it all down to me and my past mistakes?

I'm Joey Valentine and I run the motherfucking game. Except in this instance, it feels like the game is running me, and I have no idea how to stop it.

Chapter Twenty Two
Paige

"He is getting on my last fucking nerve," I shout as Donovan relays that Joey won't release the Morgan brothers unless I call him.

"I tried," Donovan says looking defeated. He hates being beaten and not getting his own way. He's not the only one. Joey seems determined to intertwine himself into my life. I need to shut this shit down.

I stand up from my desk and pick my keys up. I need to put an end to whatever mind game he is trying to play with me. He wanted my respect, he got it. He didn't ask for anything more, so I shouldn't have to be made to deal with him any longer.

"Where are you going?" Donovan asks as I walk out of my office and head down the hallway.

"I'm going to get the Morgan brothers, and to let Joey know that I'm not playing around."

***

"Paige," Raymond says as I walk through the doors of Club Valentine.

"Raymond. Joey around?" I ask, not even smiling at him.

"He's in a meeting," he informs me.

"An important one?"

"All meetings are important, Paige." Raymond smirks. "Why don't you grab a drink and go and find a seat. I'll let Joey know that you're here to see him."

He speaks to me like a silly little girl that doesn't know what to do with herself. Or at least that's how it comes across.

I nod and head to the bar, ordering a vodka and coke. I don't ever need liquid courage, but I'm pretty sure that an alcoholic drink will help keep me at ease whilst I wait for Joey to finish up with whatever he's doing. My drink is quickly placed in front of me and I take a long sip of the cool beverage.

My eyes sweep around the room. Not many people have arrived here yet, but it's still early and the real assholes don't come out to play until later. Until they have appeased their wives before picking up their side pieces who will entertain them for the evening. Ugh.

I look to the doorway that leads to the back offices, and there stands Joey, with some woman in front of him. Her back is to me, her long blond hair sweeping down her back and ending just above her ass. An ass that is barely covered. Her long legs are left bare, and her sky scraper heels give mine a run for their money. She has one of her hands on her hip, and the other is on Joey's chest. He's looking down at her, but he looks unamused. His eyes almost dead of emotion, until they look up and see me, and the fucking spark that shoots through me is like nothing else.

Joey has in front of him a blonde, who is clearly willing to do anything to get his attention, but his focus is on me. Am I fool for enjoying the power that seems to give me?

Joey seems to dismiss her and the blonde walks away, her shoulders drooping more than they were a few seconds ago. I know how it hurts to be turned away by Joey Valentine, but I doubt the woman has felt the same level of rejection as I have at the hands of the most handsome man to ever walk the fucking earth. Her pride will be hurt more than anything, whereas my heart is damaged beyond repair.

Joey nods his head to me and I take that as my cue to walk over, drink in hand, hips swaying as I go. Joey watches my every movement, something he seems to do a lot. Is it just to try and decipher everything about me so that when he comes for me I won't be able to defend myself? Or is it because he is telling the truth and he genuinely is sorry for what went down between us all those years ago?

See what you did to me Joey? You made me fucking doubt everything. I don't know what to believe anymore. I used to have it figured out, thought I was rock solid, but he's smashing apart the foundations that I built around me.

I need to hold onto my anger, channel it to push myself to the top. I did that for so long, and I need it back.

Joey holds the door open, letting me pass by him before closing it behind us. No words are exchanged as he goes ahead of me and leads me to whatever room he uses back here for business matters.

We pass by three doors until we get to the one at the very end of the hallway. Joey opens the door, moving aside once again for me to go ahead of him. When I enter the room I am momentarily blown away by the beauty of it. It's not an office as I thought it would be. It's like a mini fucking apartment in here.

To the right there are large, cream sofas, a big screen television on the wall and an electric fireplace commanding attention. The fireplace glows dimly, which goes with the low lighting and the deep purple walls. Not a colour I was expecting Joey to have chosen for his private quarters within Club Valentine.

To the left is a kitchen area with marble worktops lining the walls and a glass table in the middle of the room, four chairs sitting around it. The most impressive bit is the giant bookcase lining the back wall, hundreds of books lining the shelves.

The floor is part wooden floorboards, part carpet, and it looks every bit as plush as I would have expected, if I had had any expectations at all.

"Can I get you a refill?" Joey asks me, nodding to my half empty glass.

"No thanks," I reply as I watch him walk over to the kitchen area and open a cupboard where the glasses are kept. He takes out a tumbler and then pours himself a scotch from the lonely bottle that sits near the edge of the worktop.

He takes a sip. His lips glisten from the liquid and my mind recalls a time when I used to lick the scotch from him, tasting him and the drink all at once. It used to be one of my favourite things to do; intimate, sensual.

I quickly put the thought to the back of my mind, needing to keep my focus on the business that I came here to discuss.

"Shall we take a seat?" Joey says, already walking over to the plush sofas. I feel like I should take my shoes off, not wanting to get any dirt on the pristine cream carpet area. I don't though. If he wants me to take my shoes off, then he can damn well ask me to. He doesn't, and he sinks down onto one of the sofas. I opt to sit on the other one, facing him, not being near enough for him to touch me in any way.

"So," he begins. "You're here to talk about the Morgan brothers, I presume?"

"Who was the woman?" I say before I can stop myself.

Joey eyes almost bug out of his head at my question.

"The woman?" he asks as he sits forwards so he's on the edge of the sofa.

"Yes, the woman. The blond one who was pawing at you like a desperate feline," I say, and I can't hide the distaste in my tone.

"Desperate feline?" Joey says not bothering to hide the fucking smirk on his face. So much for showing him that I was fully in control. I can't even sit here and deny that I felt a fucking pang of jealousy at seeing the woman touch him.

"Maybe I shouldn't call her that. I mean, for all I know, she could be your girlfriend, fiancée, whatever, and the fact that you kissed me last night means that you have put me in a difficult position." I don't ever want to be the other woman, I wouldn't do that for anybody. I see it all the time. The wives that are unaware at home, thinking they've got it all. And then there are the wives that do know and decide to remain blissfully ignorant whilst being eaten alive inside with the pain that their husbands are inflicting on them.

"Paige, slow the fuck down, will you?" Joey says, amusement clear in his eyes. "I don't have a girlfriend, fiancée, or whatever," he says, mimicking my words. "And I can assure you that no one has put you in a difficult position. The woman you are referring to is of no relevance to me, other than the fact that she is the bar manager here. I have no interest in her whatsoever other than that she keeps things running smoothly."

"Oh I bet. So what is it then, just the occasional blow job under the desk?" I say, and fuck if I don't sound like a goddamn teenage girl trying to piss her high school crush off.

"If you want to talk about my dick, Paige, all you've gotta do is say the word," Joey says, chuckling.

That chuckle of his makes my sex tingle, as well as infuriating me further. I haven't come in here and asserted shit to him. All I've done is made myself a laughing stock.

"You know, this was a bad idea," I say as I stand up, ready to make my exit and run the fuck away from him again. "Just make the arrangements for the Morgan brothers to be transferred to me and our business will be concluded."

"Not so fast, Paige," Joey says as he manages to get in front of me, blocking my way to the door.

"Get out of the way, Valentine," I say, folding my arms in front of me and narrowing my eyes on him.

"Not gonna happen, babe." He chooses this moment to take a couple of steps backwards, his eyes constantly on me, and he locks the door, pocketing the key. Now if I want to get out of here I'm either going to have to wrestle him for the key or break the goddamn window.

"Joey, what are you doing?"

"You're not running from me this time, Paige. We need to talk."

"We don't need to talk about shit," I say adamantly.

"Oh, but we do," he says, a delicious smirk on his face. I can already feel myself wanting to give into him. The power of Joey. Always has been a force to be reckoned with.

"I don't have time for your games."

"I'm not playing, baby," he says as he surges forwards, coming for me. I don't move, choosing instead to stand my ground, trying to be the defiant bitch I moulded myself into. I'm not some weak-ass pussy that will drop to her knees. I won't be that woman. The one that will suck his dick at the click of his fingers. The one who will forgive all his fucking wrongs. I'm Paige fucking Roderick, and I need to show him that I am the one in control.

He wants to toy with my heart, more fool him.

He wants to try and get beneath my skin, I'll make sure he has to peel it off me piece by piece first.

I place my hand on his chest, stopping him from doing whatever the fuck he intended to. His shoulders are broad, his chest heaving, his biceps trying to distract me.

Be the stronger one, Paige. Take control, never let it go.

The games began a long time ago, but I'm about to raise the stakes. Without warning, I push up on my tip toes and press my lips to his. He wanted to be the one to take the lead, but I just turned the motherfucking tables. I can feel the tension in his body; he didn't expect me to do this. Good. Throw him off the scent, make him the fucking vulnerable one.

My tongue moves forwards, prising itself between his lips. It doesn't take more than a second for his tongue to massage mine. It doesn't even take a minute for him to lift me up, wrapping my legs around his waist. I move my hands to the nape of his neck, gripping him in place as I continue my exploration of his mouth.

He groans low and I inwardly fucking clap. He's made it clear he still wants me, and I haven't exactly hidden my want for him, but as long as I am in control, he can't get to my heart.

He moves us over to the sofas and sits down, me astride him, legs wide open for him, the skirt that I'm wearing stretching across my thighs.

His hands caress my back and my ass before moving to the inside of my thighs. He trails his fingers lightly up, goose bumps rise on my skin, and I bite his bottom lip. His growl is ferocious as I undo his shirt buttons, pushing it to the sides once all the buttons are undone. All the while I'm still moulding my mouth over his, claiming him, or so I will have him believe.

I push the shirt and jacket over his shoulders and he scoots forwards, allowing me to rid him of his clothes on his top half. The feel of his skin beneath my fingers is glorious, but I'll keep that to myself. Once this is done, I'll put it in a box and push it to the back of my memory.

He moves his lips from mine and begins to kiss my neck. It's all too familiar, too soft, too intimate and I jump up off of him until I am standing in front of him. We're both panting, and his eyes are filled with lust, want, and dare I say something more than that?

I push the thought away and undo my skirt, slowly pushing it down my legs until I am rid of it and it's in a heap on the floor. I stand here in just my knickers, bra and shoes, and Joey looks like he has hit the motherfucking jackpot.

He makes no move, just watches. He always was attentive, and I see that nothing has changed on that front.

"What's the matter, Joey?" I ask. "Don't you wanna fuck?"

He moves forward until he is standing tall in front of me.

His hands caress my face, which is far from the animal sex that I thought we would be having by now.

"You will never be just a fuck, Paige," he says before he devours my mouth, rendering me speechless. His lips are soft against mine, he's slowing the pace, and like a fucking fool I'm letting him do it.

"Stop fighting me, Paige," he whispers, his lips moving beside my ear. "You're mine, and I'm yours. Always have been, and always will be."

His words send shivers down my spine, and his lips caress my skin, trailing down my neck, along my collarbone and down to my breasts. I can't stop the feelings that he is evoking inside of me. I want him. I don't want to fight it in this moment.

I let out a soft groan as his tongue licks along my bra line. His hand pulls down the cup of my bra, and his tongue flicks across my nipple. My want for him heightens. My sex wet for him already.

His other hand cups my ass, moving around to the front and stroking me over my lace knickers.

"So fucking wet for me, Paige," he whispers, deliciously torturing me with his words and his touch.

His fingers continue to stroke, and he's on his knees in front of me. He pulls my knickers down slowly, his eyes looking hungrier by the second. I watch his reactions, his emotions, it's all there, plain as day. He never did hide what I did to him. He always made me feel empowered and like I was his reason for breathing, and he's doing it now.

His eyes flick up to meet mine and then his tongue is on me, licking, swirling and driving me absolutely wild. Honestly, seeing Joey in this position, taking me, tasting me, is the sexiest thing that I have ever seen. We always had great chemistry, a great sex life, but the years of waiting have turned this moment into something else.

I can feel the build-up gathering speed inside of me. I can feel the impending orgasm that is going to hit me sooner rather than later, and I am desperate for it.

Fuck all our problems, fuck all the complications. All that exists right now is the two of us.

My breathing quickens as Joey nudges my legs gently, making me part them a little wider, opening myself up to him a little more.

The adrenaline rush surging through me is more powerful than commanding a room full of men who are too weak to take me on.

Joey isn't weak. Joey isn't scared. Joey is the exact opposite of the assholes that I come into contact with on a daily basis, and that is why my heart doesn't want to completely give him up.

I'm lost to him as his lips close around my clit. I am dazed as his finger pushes inside of me, and I am moments away from screaming my release when he stops what he is doing and stands up, picking me up and lying me on the sofa. He unbuckles his trousers, pushing them down, along with his boxers, freeing himself and showing me how fucking hard he is for me.

In this moment we are not two of the greatest leaders in the underworld. We are not the head of our gangs, letting the pressures of having control get to us. We are not fighting against one another. We are just Joey and Paige. Two people who want to get lost in the other one.

Joey climbs on top of me, his muscular body dwarfing me. His lips connect with mine again, and I devour him, savouring every second. Gone is the restraint that I wanted to keep intact. I can't be a strong woman all of the fucking time, and with Joey's dick nudging against me, I'm damn well going to own my weak moment.

"Once we do this, Paige, I'm not letting you go," Joey says as he nibbles my ear lobe. I push my breasts against his chest, wanting the friction, enjoying the sensation of his skin making mine feel as if it is on fire.

"I want you inside of me, Joey," I say, ignoring his words and taking what I want.

My words are his undoing, and he pushes inside of me. I open up for him as he slides in, deeper and deeper, and then he starts to move back and forth. I meet him thrust for thrust as he plunges into me, sucking my nipples, making me cry out with pleasure.

I grab his ass with my hands and dig my fingers in as he fucks me harder.

"Joey," I say on a breath as I begin to tighten around him. I'm so close to the edge, desperate for him to shatter my world apart.

"Wait for me, baby."

I will myself to hold back, digging my fingers harder into his skin, but when his ice blues connect with mine, I am done for.

I cry out with the intensity of my release as Joey pounds harder, his hand moving and applying pressure to my clit at the same time.

"Oh, fuck." My shout is loud, but I don't care. I'm too lost in Joey.

His roar comes a second later, and I tighten around him some more. He continues to move, pushing me to the absolute limit before he slowly brings us both down from our high.

His lips find mine, his fingers sliding through my hair, his touch so fucking gentle that it makes me want to weep.

He's still my Joey. The one I used to know. The one that never left my heart.

He ends our kiss and nuzzles his face into my neck as the sounds of our pants fill the room.

I stare at the ceiling, allowing myself a few moments of bliss before I have to put on my big girl panties and push him away all over again. Because as much as I may want him, I'm too damn scared to let him break my heart for a second time.

Chapter Twenty Three
Joey

I have to admit, I wasn't expecting to end up with my dick buried in Paige, but this is where I'm at, and it feels fucking divine.

Paige is led beneath me, her petite body covered by mine. Her flushed face, her sparkling eyes, and her low pants have me wanting to fuck her all over again. Before the moment is lost, I lower my lips to hers and kiss her, softly, slowly, savouring every fucking second.

All of the years we wasted; me pushing her away, and her being mad at me. And here we are. Back in each other's arms. Joey and Paige. Soulmates, lovers, meant to fucking be.

She meets my tongue, stroke for stroke, and her fingers curl around my biceps. If this is what heaven feels like, then I don't want to fucking leave. I've been living in hell for so long that I don't know any different. I gave up my heaven the day I tossed her out of my life, and fuck if I don't want it back. I'm done with the games. I'm done with the bullshit. I'm done with putting on a goddamn show.

This is where I want to be. With her. Inside of her. Always beside her.

I reluctantly pull my lips from hers, and stare into her grey eyes. Eyes that have captivated me since the first moment that I saw her. Eyes that own every single part of me.

"Joey," she says, her voice no more than a whisper. "This wasn't part of the plan."

I let out a low chuckle. "It wasn't part of mine either." But I'm so fucking glad that she walked back into my life and turned the tables upside down.

"We can't do this," she says as she pushes her hands against my chest, moving me off of her, my dick sliding out of her as she scrambles away from me, moving to where her clothes lie on the floor.

The elation I felt a second ago quickly dissipates, and I sit up, watching her as she pulls her skirt on.

"Fuck," she says, grabbing her top and putting it back on, shielding her perfect form from me. Her cool façade gone, panic left in its wake.

"Paige," I say as I stand up, not worried in the slightest that I'm still fully fucking naked before her. I put my hands on her shoulders, but she shrugs me off, moving back a step, her eyes wild.

"Don't touch me," she hisses, and I wonder what the fuck happened in the space of a few seconds.

"Don't touch you?" I ask her incredulously.

The air between us intensifies. Her eyes clouding over, her walls going back up. She's shutting me back out, and damn does that send a pang to my heart.

"We shouldn't have done that," she says, running her fingers through her hair to try and rid herself of the just-fucked look.

"Why not?" I have to ask even if I won't like the answer.

"This isn't right. It's all wrong," she mutters, more to herself than to me.

"Wrong? How can what we just did be wrong?" I sound fucking weak, but I don't care. I may be a hard bastard, but when it comes to Paige, I can't do it anymore. Having a piece of her isn't enough. I want more. I want it all, and I know that she does too. I could see it in her eyes when I entered her. Never had it been clearer.

"How can it be right?" she says, confusing the hell out of me a little bit more. "I never wanted this, Joey. I never wanted to go back to what we were. I'm not just some chick you can stick it in when you need to get yourself off. I'm a fucking queen in my own right, and you're not going to take that away from me."

"I don't want to take anything away from you," I retort, pissed off that she is thinking of me in this way.

"You fuck about with feelings, Joey, and I'll be damned if you are going to fuck with mine ever again."

"Is that what this is about? About a past that I can't change? Are you forever going to punish me for the mistake I made years ago?" The anger inside of me is building.

"Punish you? Is that what you think I'm doing, Joey? Fuck, you have no idea what this is about."

"Then enlighten me," I say, my jaw clenching together.

"You want to flip shit around, make me need you, have me hanging off your every word. It will never happen." She says the last four words slowly, like she's talking to a goddamn toddler who needs it spelling out to them in plain fucking English.

"Have you lost your mind?" I say, my voice louder than a second ago. I pick my boxers up off of the floor and pull them on just for something to do. It's either that or ploughing my fist into the wall in anger.

"Yes," she says. "For a moment there, I did, but it sure as shit won't happen again."

She stalks away from me, going to my trousers and digging in the pocket, producing the key that I tucked in there when I locked the door.

"Is that it? Are we done here?" I ask her, my arms held out either side of me, my pride and my heart taking a fucking knock.

She gets to the door, puts the key in and I hear the click of the lock opening. Her hand rests on the handle as she turns her head to me, her eyes glazing over with unshed tears.

"We're done," she confirms. "You're not good for me, Joey. You use people, hurt them, and when they are irrelevant to your life, you cut them loose. I'm not Paige Daniels anymore, Joey, and I never will be again."

She goes to open the door but freezes at my next words.

"I meant it when I said that I wasn't letting go."

Her sad smile has my anger fading and my heart ripping in two. "It's time that you did."

She walks out, the door closing softly behind her, and I fall to my knees. She's the only woman alive that could make me fall, and I just fucking lost her.

Chapter Twenty Four
Paige

Joey released the Morgan brothers to me an hour ago.

Donovan, Rome and Bray went to get them.

It's been two days since Joey and I took things too far, and we haven't spoken since.

I've showered countless times to try and wash away the feel of his hands on my skin. I don't want to think about his touch and how it had me wanting to revert back to the old Paige. The one that was so in love with him she would have done anything to keep him.

I've kept my mind busy, being more assertive than normal, more demanding with my boys, and more of a fucking bitch. Heart of stone, blood as cold as ice. That's me, and there is no room for anything else.

I've been running on empty for forty eight hours. Barely slept, worked out in my home gym until I couldn't feel my fucking legs, and eaten no more than a few crumbs because I can't stomach the thought of much else right now.

I let Joey see me. I let him in, even if it was only for a short while. A game of chess, and I ended up being the pawn. I came here to be the queen, ready to checkmate the fucking king, and I'm failing.

"Boss," Donovan says as he stands in my office doorway, his voice pulling me from my thoughts.

"They ready for me?" I ask him.

He nods his head and I slowly rise. I'm dressed in my black trousers, navy blue sleeveless shirt, and my usual killer stilettos. And I'm about to unleash a whole world of fury on the fucking Morgan brothers. Neither of them gave up Bobby's whereabouts to Joey and his men, so now it's my turn. They should have been with me all along, but then that would have been plain sailing, something that Joey seems incapable of doing.

I move my neck from side to side, rolling my shoulders as I make my way to Donovan.

"You okay, Paige?" Donovan asks, and I stop in my tracks.

"I'm fine." I bristle at his question.

"You might be able to fool the other boys, Paige, but not me," he says as he lays a hand on my forearm. I let my eyes follow his fingers as they gently wrap around me. It feels wrong, like I'm doing something that I shouldn't be, and I pull away from him as if I have been burned.

Joey is in my head, consuming every single part of me. I need to get him the fuck out before I crumble.

I can't crumble.

I didn't come here to lose the fight.

Donovan frowns at me, but I just pull my shoulders back and fix him with my stare.

"I'm not trying to fool anyone, Donovan, and I don't need to explain myself to anyone either. I'm running the fucking show, and I don't appreciate you questioning me."

"I'm not questioning you, Paige, I'm concerned for you," he says, and I wonder why Donovan has come over all fucking soppy. He doesn't do concern anymore. Last time he showed real concern was the day he picked me up off the street, but since then, he's been hard, unforgiving, and showed me to look out for no one but yourself. It's why we always got along so well, and why he is my right hand man. Because we take no shit, and we certainly don't mollycoddle each other with soppy-ass questions that verge on having to discuss feelings.

I take a step towards him, my eyes narrowing ever so slightly. "We don't show concern, Donovan. Isn't that the first rule you ever taught me? Show them nothing and then they have nothing to play with?"

He nods.

"Isn't the second rule to never ever feel like you have to give them an explanation?"

Another nod.

"And isn't the third rule to put a bullet in the head of the person that asks those questions and won't let them fucking go?"

His gulp is noticeable, but I know that he isn't scared. He doesn't do scared. I have no idea what the gulp is for, and I don't fucking care.

"Now, if you're done asking me ridiculous questions, do you want to join me in scaring the shit out of these brothers?" I say as I feel a smirk tug at my lips.

"Would love nothing more," Donovan replies. He's always up for a bit of retribution, and the Morgan brothers are about to get it in spades.

"Good. Let's go and have some fun," I say as I lead the way to the basement where the jackasses are tied up, waiting to see what fate has in store for them.

I'm going to enjoy taking my frustrations out of them.

Just two more assholes off of the streets.

It won't stop the rest of them out there, but it will give me peace of mind that these two are never getting out of here alive.

Chapter Twenty Five
Joey

For the first time in my life, I feel like I'm going out of my damn mind.

All I can think about is her. I can smell her scent around me, on me. I can hear her voice and see her when I close my eyes.

Paige fucking Daniels. Yes, I said Daniels, because that is who she is, and that is who she will always be. She's just hiding beneath a cover. I need to find a way to coax her out, get her back, make her mine.

As I drive my car to the tip off that I have been given about Bobby fucking Morgan, I have to stop myself from thinking about my head between her legs, my tongue on her clit, and my dick in her pussy. I thought I had her back. I thought that I had climbed those damn walls and knocked the fuckers down, but of course that would be too easy. Paige is nothing if not a force to be reckoned with, and I'm going to do all of the reckoning that I can.

I've given her a couple of days, and I'll give her as many more as she needs until she realises that the only place to be is with me. And I know that she is going to fight me every step of the way, but I'll fight back harder. I gave her up once. Never again.

I pull up by the side of the canal path, turning the car off and waiting for Big Danny, Simon and Pascal to catch up with me. I drove alone, and Big Danny is driving the other car, bringing up the rear. I didn't want company. I wanted time to myself. Lord knows I can't get a fucking minutes peace anywhere else right now. Bobby being missing is putting doubt on what the fuck I can do. He's side-stepped me for too long.

I am aware that the Morgan brothers are Paige's battle, but when she asked me to help, she brought me the fuck in. I can't have people questioning whether I am incapable of serving up the damn goods.

My goal to get out of this motherfucking world of crime and punishment is getting further away from me, but the pull of Paige doesn't make that seem so bad anymore. My reason for leaving has changed. It was to leave it all behind, make a fresh start, maybe find Paige and settle down. But she's in this world now, and there is no way in hell that she will run these streets without me by her side.

I should have trusted her with my secrets all those years ago. I should have put faith in us, but I didn't. And now I have to make up for that, even if it takes me a fucking lifetime.

I see Big Danny pull the car up behind mine, and I get out, sliding on my shades and buttoning up my suit jacket. I came dressed to kill, literally. I have no interest in letting Bobby live. If Paige wants to get revenge on me for taking the kill from her, then so be it. Like I said before, I will fight for her, and I will fight against her in order to keep her in my goddamn life. Makes me sound fucking crazy, but whatever.

"You ready?" I say as Pascal walks up to me.

"Yes, boss." He nods, and the other two mimic him.

"Good. We are ten minutes away from his supposed hiding hole. Keep your eyes open, ears pricked, and don't let the bastard get away," I tell them. I'm determined to nail this asshole to the wall.

I turn and start to walk, the crunch of my feet on the gravel pissing me off. It's too noisy already, but I'll move onto the grass verge when I get closer to the tip off.

We walk for five minutes, and then I see the lonely canal boat up ahead. That is my mark. I swiftly move onto the grass and the others follow suit. They've already been prepped, I have no need to remind them of the protocol.

I close in, keeping as quiet as I can. I jump across the canal path to land on the other side avoiding the gravel. There is no one else around, and as I come to the back of the canal boat, I crouch down. I move along, looking in one of the small windows that is edged in moss. The chipped paintwork and the rundown look of the boat makes me think that we have the right place. Bobby was always a dirty fucker, in life and in hygiene.

I'm almost on my knees as I round the front of the boat, Pascal behind me, Big Danny waiting at the rear with Simon. My hand is placed on my gun as I hear footsteps on the other side of the boat. I crouch lower, I wait, I keep my eyes trained on the other side of the boat so that when the fucker reveals himself, he will have the shock of his life.

Another footstep and I draw my gun.

Another, and I click the safety off.

One more and I get the shock of my fucking life.

"Looks like you're late to the party, boys." The smirk on her face, the way her eyes sparkle, her long legs in those leather fucking trousers, and her hair tumbling down, framing her face. Paige fucking Daniels beat us to our mark, and I sure as shit am not going to complain.

Chapter Twenty Six
Paige

The look of shock on all of their faces is priceless.

"What took you guys so long?" I goad, knowing that me finding Bobby's hiding place first will be pissing them off. Good. It was my fucking mark anyway.

"Nice play," Joey says as he stands to his full height, towering tall, looking every inch the man I want to fuck but can't. His words nearly knock me off my game. *Nice play?*

"It's amazing how quickly you can find someone when you get the right people to talk," I say, raising one eyebrow, hitting home that he couldn't get the Morgan brothers to squeal on Bobby.

Joey raises his eyebrow in return and I can't help my smile.

"You can go, boys," Joey instructs his minions without turning to look at them. His eyes are solely focussed on me. The boys do as they are told and scurry away, no questions asked. I would expect nothing less from them at this point. Word on the street is that Joey is one of the best underworld bosses to work for. Once you've cracked your way into his crew, you're set for life, assuming you don't die in the process of course.

Joey waits until their footsteps fade away.

Neither of us say a word.

We drink each other in, and I can't help but have a flashback of us, in his office, fucking on the sofa, his hands roaming over my body...

I mentally shrug the images off. I don't need to be distracted by the thought of his toned abs and his rock hard dick. I'm here to finish business, and then I'll never have to deal with Joey fucking Valentine again. It will be my personal mission to stay the hell away from him.

I no longer have an interest in taking him down. It will come with time. I'm already on a fucking par with him anyway.

It has been my mission to dethrone him for so long, but I can't allow myself to do it. I can't allow myself to be tangled up with Joey. My heart will be the one to get broken, and I won't let anyone break it again. Once was enough.

"So, how did you find out about Bobby's hideout?" Joey asks, breaking the silence.

"Now, now, Joey, you know that we don't kiss and tell."

His eyes light up at the word kiss. Fuck. He's looking at me like he wants to devour me, right here, right now. My sex begins to tingle. *No, Paige, back it the fuck up.*

"If I tell you my secrets, then you'll know how to hit me hard, and I can't allow you to do that," I say, needing to get the hell off this boat and the fuck away from Joey before I cave to my womanly urges and straddle him, right here, not giving a fuck who sees us.

"Who says I want to hit you hard, Paige?" he questions, his eyes burning into mine.

"Wasn't that always the goal?"

"I'm done playing games. I thought I made that clear the other day, in my office." His voice is low, and it does things to me. Things that it shouldn't.

"I'm not doing this with you, Joey," I say as I step forward and aim to walk past him, but he wraps his fingers around my arm. My eyes connect with his ice blues, and damn if I don't turn back into Paige Daniels for just a second.

"And I'm not fucking around, Paige," Joey grits out, our lips so close that all I would have to do is push forward and our passion would be ignited all over again. "You seem to think that I have an agenda here, and I have no idea how to convince you that I don't."

"Oh, please, Joey Valentine always has an agenda," I say as I bite my bottom lip, my toes curling from the heat between us.

"Not with you," he says, and time just stops. It's just us. Joey and Paige. Ex-lovers trying to figure out their shit.

I don't want to be her.

I don't want to be the Daniels chick that let a man be her downfall.

I don't want to show weakness.

I've built myself up to be a cold hearted bitch who won't stand for anything other than obedience.

I've built those walls, and fucking Joey is knocking them down, again.

I let him slither through the cracks the other night. Can I really let him slither in some more?

My heart wants to. My heart is the one place that has never really let him go.

My head tells me to remain strong.

But what do you do when those two things are at war with one another?

Do you give in?

Do you fight back?

Do you allow yourself another chance of happiness?

Do you open yourself up to potential heartbreak? Or do you let it all go and move the fuck on with your life?

I move my head, placing my lips beside Joey's ear as I whisper, "Prove it," before I shrug my arm free from his grip and walk away.

Chapter Twenty Seven
Paige

"We need to act fast," I say to Donovan, Rome, Bray and Tony. "We are two men down, so we need to work harder."

Miles is still recovering from the stabbing, and Trevor is still holed up with Grace in my house. I can't risk them going anywhere until Bobby is found.

I lied when I told Joey that he was late to the party. It turns out that I was too. Bobby had done a bunk, been tipped off, knew we were coming for him, and I need to find out how he knew.

The other Morgan brothers are barely hanging onto their lives. I've done everything that I can think of to get them to talk, and now I'm resorting to my last bartering tool. The one thing that will show whether they are loyal or whether they are the fucking lowest of the low that we all believe them to be.

"Bray, you, Rome and Tony will go and get Meghan Morgan."

"Do we know where she is?" Bray asks, ready to get the fuck on with the job. I can always count on him to be the one to get stuck in first.

"She's working at Morgan's." I roll my eyes at the originality of the name. Morgan's is a restaurant owned by the three brothers. My sources tell me that Meghan has no ownership stake in the place, she just works there as the front of house, if that is what you can call her job title. It's hardly the fucking Ritz. More like the pits.

Meghan has been working there ever since she left school aged sixteen. She's now twenty-nine. No home of her own, no husband or boyfriend, and no real friends to speak of. She's like the Morgan brothers lacky, and she was also the one driving the getaway car when Miles was stabbed. I had to re-watch the security tapes about a thousand times to come to that conclusion. She tried to hide her identity, but she should have done a better job. It might have taken me a while to figure it out, but I always do eventually, and my confrontation with this bitch is overdue. I haven't informed my boys of this piece of information yet, so it will be a nice surprise for them when I cut her at the throat.

Even though the brothers make out that they would do anything to protect Meghan, my guess is that they don't want anything to interfere with the setup they've got going on.

I'm about to fuck that shit up.

They don't deserve to have a nice little setup. Not after everything they have done.

"She there now?" Bray asks, looking at the watch in his wrist.

"She is, and she will be there until eleven thirty tonight, but we're obviously going to have her back here before then." It's not a request. It is a must-do. They can't let her get away from them. She will have been trained to stay alert for any signs of danger, and my guys need to get in there quick, smooth and bring her back here for me to end this goddamn game of hide and seek.

"Sure thing, boss," Bray says before beckoning the other two to follow him out of the room.

That just leaves me and Donovan. He watches me, and I arch an eyebrow.

"You're really bringing her into this?" he asks.

"Why wouldn't I bring her into this?" I reply.

"Because she isn't the issue here."

"She's a Morgan, and she might just be the fucking answer to the question we've been asking."

He looks pissed off with my answer, but I couldn't care less. The Morgan brothers have taken up too much of my time as it is. I don't want to waste much more on them.

"Is this about getting one up on Joey?" Donovan asks, and there it is. The question that he really wants the answer to, and it all goes back to Joey Valentine. He's been prodding for days, wanting to know the real ins and outs. He knows me, so he knows there is more than what I have told him, but it is absolutely none of his fucking business.

"Finding out where Bobby is has nothing to do with Joey," I say, stressing each word. "If you remember, I originally went to Joey for help, so no, Valentine has fuck all to do with this."

"You haven't been the same since you started speaking to him," Donovan informs me, as if I fucking asked him to share his opinion.

"And what exactly have I been doing differently?" I'm genuinely intrigued to know so that I can fucking change it.

"You're going soft, Paige."

I laugh at him. His response is ridiculous. "I am not going soft."

"If you're not going soft, then why aren't you forging ahead with your plan of going after him?" Donovan asks. I told him, and only him, that I was dropping my vendetta against Joey, something I thought he would be pleased about, but apparently not.

"I told you, I'm done playing Valentine's games. They're pointless, a waste of my time, and I have no intention of engaging with him."

"Bullshit. You love playing games, Paige. I've watched you run rings around men like Joey before, and you have never pulled the plug on a fucking target." Donovan is right. I haven't pulled the plug on anyone but Joey, and it's doing nothing but opening up a can of worms that I could do without.

"I no longer have an interest in taking what he has," I say with a shrug of my shoulders.

"Still not buying it."

"Well it's all you're getting," I retort.

"That's not how we do things, Paige. It's always been me and you against the rest. Why the fuck are you shutting me out now?" Donovan says, his voice raising ever so slightly.

"Since when did you become such a fucking drama queen, Donovan?" I goad.

"Don't answer a question with a question, just be honest with me," Donovan says, and I can see the worry in his eyes that I am keeping secrets, but they are mine to keep, and keep them I will.

"I don't know how many times I can tell you this before you start to believe me, but there is nothing to know about Joey Valentine," I say between clenched teeth. Donovan is pissing me off, and so is Joey and he isn't even here.

"You keep playing that record, Paige, and one day I might not be here to listen to the truth," Donovan says, his jaw ticking, his arms folded across his chest.

I step closer to him, my eyes narrowing.

"You threatening to abandon me?" I ask.

"Total trust. We've always had it. It's why we have come so far in such a short amount of time. If we don't have that, there is no point in me and you anymore."

"I trust you as much as I need to."

"That's bullshit, Paige and you know it," he retaliates.

"Never trust anybody."

"Except for me," he says, his arms going out either side of him. "Don't act like you don't, it's insulting."

His words, they ring true.

But I can't voice the words that I need to.

I've always told myself that I will only trust as much as I need to, and as much as I kid myself, I know, deep down, that I have trusted Donovan more than anyone, since Joey.

But no matter how much I have to admit to myself that Donovan does have my trust, I can't let him think that his threats are going to make me talk.

There are some things I need to keep to myself, and Joey being part of my past is one of them.

"If you're doubting me, then you better turn around and walk out that door right now," I say, not backing down.

Time ticks by, the tension growing thicker by the second.

When a couple of minutes have ticked by, I smirk. "Yeah, that's what I thought," I say as I brush past him and leave the room. Donovan won't go anywhere. He's always had my back.

If that's the case, then why are you worrying?

I storm out of the house, grabbing my car keys as I slam the front door shut behind me. I need to unleash some of my frustration. I need an outlet, and there is only one place in the world that I can do that right now.

It's time for me to start facing up to my feelings.

Ignoring them is only fucking my shit up.

I had it all figured out, until Joey played his hand and put his fucking cards on the table.

Joey Valentine, my goddamn downfall, and the only one that has the power to break everything that I have so carefully crafted.

And I don't even want him to give up that power. It's not about that anymore. It's not about winning, losing or seeking revenge.

He's made it clear that we're equals, neither one of us better than the other.

The question is, do I keep playing by my rules? Or do I change the game and allow myself to go after the very thing that I have denied myself since the moment that I laid my eyes back on Joey?

Play by the rules or change the game?

Fuck.

No one ever said that love was easy.

Chapter Twenty Eight
Joey

Another day, another asshole taught a valuable lesson.

I just spent the last hour schooling some prick about respect.

Nobody fucks with me, and some don't believe it until they learn the hard way.

I don't relish the idea of kicking someone's ass, but when it's called for, I will fucking bring it. And bring it I did. Whether it was more enforced because of my frustration over Paige lately, I'm not sure, but I can guarantee that motherfucker won't be bothering me again.

Lewis Knox, stupid man. Twenty-three years old, thinks he's running at the top of his game, thinks he can come into my playground and take shit from me without paying the price. He's been trying to sidestep me for weeks, but I can safely say that he has gotten the message that he can't do that without severe consequences. His face is going to take a while to heal. As for his mind, I can't say that he will ever fully recover, but they don't call me the motherfucking King of this world for nothing.

This is why I wanted out. I wanted to get away from all the shadiness, the mind games, the crucifixions. I wanted a normal life, where no one knew me, where I would be free to do what I liked, see who I liked and live a peaceful existence.

I was nearly there, getting ready to hand over the reins to Raymond. And then Paige came back into my life.

Her words come back to me. *"Prove it."*

Prove it.

Prove it.

Prove it.

I've been racking my brains for a way to show her that I am in this for the long haul, and that if I have to live in this corrupt underworld forever with her, then so be it. But I fear that she will always doubt me.

I could lay all my fucking cards on the table, and she could tear them up, claim that it was a false deal.

With a sigh, I walk over to the small bar area in my office, picking up a bottle of scotch and pouring it into a tumbler, watching the liquid slide over the ice cubes that were already in there when I walked in here. My guys know me well, and I have no doubt that Raymond put the ice cubes in the tumbler, knowing that the first thing I would need after a beat down was a glass of scotch on the rocks.

I raise the glass to my lips, ready to take a sip, savour the taste, feel the burn, when my office door flies open. My eyes flick up, and I'm ready to tear whoever is bursting in here a new asshole, until I see the shoes. Stilettos. Red ones. My eyes roam up, and I see the tight jeans hugging her curves. Moving up a little more, I see her red, lace top, clinging to her like a second skin. Her hair tumbling around her in waves, her lips red and full, her stormy grey eyes blazing.

Paige. My fucking Paige.

She kicks the door shut, her breathing heavy, her fists clenched.

I slowly put the tumbler down.

I wait.

She came to me, this is her show, not mine.

The ball is in her court. She's the one running things. I'm just hoping to be taken along for the ride.

She takes a few steps forward, her heels clicking on the wooden floorboards.

"Did you mean it, Joey?" she asks, her voice small, almost as if she is unsure of herself.

I remain quiet, waiting for her to give me more.

Another click of her heel.

"Are you really going to prove it to me?" Another question, still I give no response.

Click, click, click.

Her feet stop when she gets to the other side of the bar, her hands going out either side of her as she leans on the bar top, palms down, shoulders raised slightly.

I remain like a fucking statue.

"Am I really yours?" she purrs, and fuck if her words don't make my inner animal want to come out. I could devour her, right here, right now, and I don't think for one minute that she would stop me. Not in this moment. Not at this time.

My hands are resting just in front of hers. All I would have to do is move them forward an inch to touch her.

"Could you imagine someone else taking your place?" she whispers, and my jaw clenches. "Could you imagine another man touching what you say is yours?"

Fuck no.

Never going to happen.

"Could you fuck another woman like you fuck me?"

Again, no, and I don't like where these fucking questions are going. What is she doing? Goading me? Testing me?

I have no fucking clue, but her next question almost shatters me.

"If I let you in, are you going to break my heart again?" Her quiet voice fades off a little more with each word, and I can no longer stand here and do nothing.

My hand moves, my fingers entwining with her hair where my hand stops at the back of her head.

"You gonna make me cry again, Joey?" she whispers, and the tremble of her lip has my other hand covering hers.

This is the first time that she has really let me see the true Paige, the one I fell in love with and never let go. This is the woman that Paige Roderick is hiding. She thinks that Paige Daniels is weak, but what she fails to see is that they are both the same fucking person, and they each have my fucking heart.

Her eyes filling with unshed tears leaves me speechless, so I do the only thing that I can in this moment to convey everything that I am feeling. I kiss her. It's not quick, it's not animalistic, it's not frenzied. It's slow, passionate and emotional.

Her lips move against mine, her silent tears falling down her cheeks. I cup her face and use my thumbs to wipe them away. Her muffled groan has me wanting to fill her, to let her know that I'm right here with her, beside her.

"Don't cry, baby," I say as I brush my lips across hers, not wanting to move away.

"I don't want to be this person, Joey," she says, still her voice a whisper. "I can't do it again."

"Neither can I," I tell her truthfully. Letting her go the first time fucking broke me. We may both put on a front, one which looks like it can't be penetrated, but we both know it's a lie. We can fool other people, but not each other.

This is her walls breaking down, letting me in, showing me a slither of the fucking pain that I caused her. I thought that pushing her away was right. I thought that I was saving her from a world of pain. But what I actually did was damage her heart, and I'm going to do everything that I can to repair the damage that I caused.

Seeing her hurting, seeing her tears, seeing the fear in her eyes, I don't want any of that. I want to see her happy, I want to be the one that she trusts above all others in this world, and I won't stop until I have made her believe in me, in us.

I let her go for a second as I round the bar, so I can hold her flush to my chest.

Her grey eyes look up at me, willing me to be honest with her, and that's exactly what I'm going to be.

One of my hands lay at the base of her spine, the other gripping her hip.

"Paige, letting you go was the biggest mistake of my life. Learning to live without you was damn near impossible. I've already told you that I thought it was for the best, to get you away from this world, to spare you from becoming a target for anyone that wanted to get to me. I made a choice, and I was wrong.

"I know that you doubt me, and I know that it's going to take time to rebuild the trust that we once had, but make no mistake when I say this, you are mine. You have my heart. You are the woman for me, always have been and always will be.

"I don't want you to hurt anymore. I don't want to see you cry because of the hurt that I caused you. And I don't want to play fucking mind games. I want you, Paige. I want it all. I want the house, the kids, the fucking dog running round the garden, and I want it with you.

"There hasn't been anyone else, Paige."

"No one?" she asks, her eyes wide.

"No one," I confirm. I couldn't bring myself to touch another woman after her. Sure, I've had countless women try, but it never felt right, and I simply wasn't interested.

"You know, you're not as much of a hard-ass as people think," she says injecting a little humour into her voice.

154

I chuckle. "You're the only one that will ever get to see this side of me." No one else deserves to see the soft side of Joey Valentine.

"Have you got work to do?" she asks me, biting that juicy bottom lip of hers.

"Nothing that can't wait."

"You wanna get out of here?" she asks.

Do I want to get out of here?

What kind of question is that?

Fuck, yes, I want to get out of here.

"You coming with me?" I ask, needing her to confirm what I'm thinking even after I just poured my heart out to her.

I swear, time fucking stops as I wait for her answer.

"Yes."

And just like that we're Joey and Paige again.

Not Valentine and Roderick.

Just plain old girl meets boy. Man loves woman. Lovers reunited.

Chapter Twenty Nine
Paige

I may have lost my damn mind in the last twenty minutes, but I'm surprisingly okay with that.

After Donovan questioned me about Joey, I knew that I was never going to be able to let him go. Joey Valentine has always been my number one. Sure, I may want to challenge him, push him, and make him go a little crazy, but that's all part of what makes us, us.

I've tried to fight what I feel for Joey, but I'm fighting a losing battle. I'll always want him, always love him and will always want him to want me.

We were a whirlwind once before, so God knows what kind of force we will be now.

I'm meant to be waiting at my house for the boys to bring Meghan fucking Morgan to me, but in this moment, I couldn't give a toss. All I want is to be near Joey, to feel him touching me, to lose myself in how he makes me feel.

I can still be a strong woman even with Joey on my damn arm. I don't need to lose sight of who I have become. I don't know why I ever thought that he would want to take the crown that I have worked so fucking hard for.

Sure, we've had our moments of goading one another, trying to force the other one to show their hand early on in the game, but I'm done with it. I'm ready to give him another chance, to explore what we once could have been.

Giving up is no longer an option.

Taking him down is not even in my agenda. I no longer have an agenda when it comes to him.

I just want to be Paige. A woman who wants a man, and there ain't no one more manly than Joey Valentine.

We've just arrived at his house. He's unlocking the front door, and even his fucking back is sexy. Dear God, it's like I've opened up all of my girlie fucking thoughts and there is no way to shut them down right now. The girl in love that I once was has been shut down for so long that I fear I may maul him to death taking my fill of him. I don't think Joey would complain though, not if the way he is looking at me is any indication.

His eyes are trained on me as I walk past, swinging my hips from side to side a little more than is necessary.

I own every moment, and I sure as fuck am going to own this one.

He shuts the door, turns to me, and smiles.

I almost kick myself for my knees going momentarily weak at that damn smile, but I remind myself that I am allowed moments like this.

I may be a fucking force, but I'm also a bloody human. I have feelings. I have needs. I have wants. And Joey is every fucking thing that I crave. Powerful, exquisite, dangerous, handsome, charming, he's the whole package. And I want to unwrap that package, make him mine, and be his fucking equal.

I take a step towards him, and he takes one towards me. I barely take in the décor of the hallway that we are standing in, because none of that is on my radar. Joey is all consuming, filling the space like no one else can.

We may have fucked in his office the other night, and that may have roused things inside of me, but I have a feeling that nothing is going to prepare me for what is about to come.

He holds his hand out to me, and I take it.

The tingles that shoot up my arm quickly make their way through my body and end up between my legs.

He pulls me against his chest. His rock hard chest.

He uses his other hand to tip my chin up, so that I am looking at him.

His eyes blaze with every emotion possible. Want, need, excitement, fear, love. *Yeah, I'm right there with you, baby.*

The tension surrounding us is off the scale.

This is the two most powerful people in the underworld coming together as one. The leaders solidifying their place in each other's lives.

His head dips down, his lips hover over mine, his breath feathers across my skin.

And I shudder with delight when he brushes those lips over mine before taking them in a bruising kiss. His hands snake around my waist, my hands hold onto his broad shoulders. His slight stubble grazes against my delicate skin, and I couldn't love the feel of it more. Joey is going to leave his mark on me, again, and I'm ready for it.

His hands slide to my ass, and he lifts me up, allowing me to wrap my legs around his waist. Then he starts to walk, and he could be taking me out to the fucking garden for all I care right now, but it seems that he has chosen to go upstairs. Our lips stay connected, my fingers tug on his hair, his growl has me hungry for more.

He kicks a door open and I hold on tighter as he lowers me, his body over mine, until I land on a soft surface. His bed.

Our lips break apart and he stands back up, towering over me. My legs are still wrapped around him as he takes off his suit jacket, throwing it to the floor. His fingers move to his shirt buttons, and he slowly undoes each one. In fact, it seems to take a fucking age for him to reveal his rock hard abs, and I struggle not to take over and hurry him the fuck up.

When his shirt joins his jacket in a heap on the floor, I allow my eyes to trail the hard lines of his body. I prop myself up on my elbows so that I can get a good look at the fucking God stood in front of me.

His hands move to his trousers, he undoes the button, and I lick my lips in anticipation of seeing his cock again. The bulge in his pants already tells me that he's hard. For me. For us. For what we are about to do.

As he pushes his clothes down his legs, I can no longer sit back. I want in on the action, right now. I sit up and move forwards, taking his dick in my mouth before he realises what I'm doing.

"Fuck," he says, abandoning his removal of clothes, his hand going to the back of my head, caressing it gently.

I slide his dick in and out of my mouth, swirling my tongue, sucking a little harder each time I go up and down. I move slowly, torturously so, marvelling in the moans coming from him.

I move a little faster, wanting to ignite his passion to the max.

And it appears I do just that when he pulls my head back, releasing his cock from my mouth, his eyes blazing into mine. I lick my lips and am pushed onto my back and stripped of my clothes quicker than ever before. Lying fully naked before him, he lifts one of my legs and removes my stiletto before doing the same to the other leg. The act is so fucking sexy, but then it gets even sexier when he places his lips on my ankle and kisses a trail all the way up to the inside of my thigh.

Joey's face between my legs, fucking beautiful.

He parts my legs wider, leaving me spread eagled and completely at his mercy, and when his tongue darts out, hitting my sweet spot, I feel like I might self-combust.

I forgot how fucking good he was at eating pussy.

His tongue, his lips, his moves, it's all so fucking good.

My back arches off of the bed and his hands come up, caressing my breasts, tweaking my nipples. I am in pleasure heaven.

My toes curl as I teeter on the edge of release. My breathing quickens, my groans get louder. And just when I am about to let go and fully fucking relish in how amazing it all feels, Joey stops everything. I blink for a few seconds, wondering what the fuck just happened. I lift my head to see where the hell he went to, and there he is, looking at me like I am his fucking world.

If I wasn't in deep before, then I sure am now. I know that look. I've seen that look before.

Joey is about to claim me, for good this time.

He crawls up my body until his face is above mine.

He settles between my legs, his length nudging against my opening.

His eyes, oh his eyes. Those ice blues looking straight into my stormy greys, showing me that this is going to be the moment where I need to let go and give myself to him fully. This is the moment when I really have to choose. This is where he wants me to tell him that this is for real, no games, no foul play.

"I'm ready, Joey," I tell him, not even having to think about it. "I've been ready all along, it just took me a little while to see it."

"I'm not letting you go again, Paige, so just know that if you run, I will chase. If you put those walls back up, I will knock them down. And if you shut me out, I'll come blazing in like the goddamn sun."

Fuck.

"This is real," I start as I place my hands on either side of his face. "No games, no agendas. I want this, I want you,

Joey. The queen beside the king, as it always should have been."

"Damn fucking straight," he says before taking my mouth with his and sliding his dick into me.

He fills me, swallowing my moans as his tongue moves against mine.

He moves in and out of me slowly.

He's in no rush, and neither am I.

My orgasm builds, my pleasure heightens, and I tighten around him.

His lips move away as his forehead rests against mine.

"I don't ever want to be without you again, Paige," he whispers as I continue to shoot towards my release. "I missed you, baby, so fucking much."

"Joey," I say on a breath, his words pushing me to the brink.

His thumb finds my clit, and he slowly moves it in circles.

And I am fucking done for.

I cry out as I hit my peak. I cry out some more as Joey hits his. We both ride it out, prolonging the pleasure, needing to savour every single second of it.

My body trembles from the aftermath.

My mind floats on cloud fucking nine.

And my heart beats fast for the man led on top of me.

Joey fucking Valentine. Mine.

Chapter Thirty
Paige

Dear God, I can't move. My legs don't want to work as I attempt to get off of the bed.

Joey is asleep next to me. I must have drifted off after he fucked me a second time. The first time was claiming each other. The second one was pure animal sex. I'm damn sure I marked his back with my fingernails as they drove into his skin whilst he milked every bit of my orgasm from me.

So fucking good.

I smile at the vivid memory that I get to keep forever.

I gingerly stand up, making sure that my legs will actually hold me up after Joey's reminder of what he can do to me.

I carefully tip-toe across the room so that I don't wake him and search the hall way for the toilet so that I can freshen up before I have to leave and deal with Meghan fucking Morgan. I hope that for her sake she gives up the information that I want easily. I don't have the energy to fight her for every little detail.

As I walk down the hall way, I peek in each door, trying to find the bathroom, and of course, it's hidden at the very end, behind the last door that I come to.

I walk in to the sheer extravagance, but then I wouldn't expect anything else from Joey. He probably hired the most expensive interior designer when he decorated this place. From the gleaming gold taps to the massive walk in shower, it is like something out of a show home.

Looking at my reflection in the mirror, I can already notice the sparkle in my eyes, the flush of my cheeks and how the tension lines have disappeared from my forehead. It seems that giving into my desire for Joey is already having an impact, even if it was only a couple of hours ago. I've battled so hard, and for so long, but maybe giving up the battle to keep Joey out is going to be the making of me. I sure hope so because I really wouldn't survive the heartbreak again.

The bathroom door opens behind me, and Joey's eyes connect with mine in the mirror.

His heated gaze almost boring into me.

My body heats from that alone.

He moves towards me, slowly, like a predator, and I'm more than happy to be his prey.

He stops behind me. His hands gently rest on my hips. Goose-bumps ignite all over me.

His touch alone has me wanting more.

"I thought for a second that maybe you had left," he says, his voice low, his head moving down, his lips grazing the skin of my shoulder.

"Don't worry, big guy, I'm still here," I say with a smile on my face, our eyes connected in the mirror.

"Big guy, it's been a long time since I heard those words."

It was my pet name for him, back when we were first together. Big guy. In more ways than one.

His hands move around to my front, and his right hand lightly trails down, further and further, until he is parting me before my very eyes. I watch mesmerised as his finger circles my clit, enticing a moan from deep within me. I close my eyes as he continues to circle, only for him to put his lips by my ear and whisper, "Open your eyes, baby. Watch as I make you come undone."

And damn, my eyes pop straight open, and I watch.

I watch as he pleasures me.

I watch as he the king brings the queen to her knees.

And I love every single second of it.

Raw.

Passionate.

Real.

Just the two of us, no drama, no hate, and nothing but a fucking lifetime of making up to do. But I have to cut the party short, because a queen's work is never done.

"I gotta go, Joey," I say, when I get my breath back.

"You sure about that?" he says as he nibbles on my ear lobe and fuck if I don't want to just throw in the towel and let him devour me over and over again. But I can't. I have people depending on me, and I have to get answers to the questions that are plaguing my mind.

"Afraid so, big guy."

"Anything I can help with?" he asks, still nibbling.

Jesus Christ, if he doesn't stop doing that, I'll never get out of here.

"Joey," I say a little more sternly, and he stops, letting out a sigh as he does.

"You can't expect to be naked and me do nothing about it," he says, a cheeky smirk on his face.

"All in good time, big guy, all in good time," I say as I saunter past him and head back to his bedroom.

"I fucking love it when you call me that," I hear him say and it brings a smile to my face.

Me too, big guy. Me too.

Chapter Thirty One
Paige

"Where is she?" I ask as I walk through my front door, kicking it shut behind me.

"Downstairs, boss," Bray answers.

"She tried to pull anything?" I ask, needing to know whether she is erratic or calm as fuck, so that I have an inkling of how all of this is going to go down.

"No problems. Came willingly. Didn't even bat an eyelid," Bray informs me.

Huh.

Interesting.

"Donovan down there with her?"

"Yes, boss."

"Okay. Well, let's get this show started then," I say as I head along the hall way and make my way downstairs to the basement where the fucking low lives are kept.

Each click of my heel becomes louder the further down I go, until I am at the bottom and I see Donovan stood at the end, his arms folded, legs parted, looking every inch the badass that I know he is.

Tony is stood along from him, beside the cage that contains the two brothers. And then sat on a chair, her arms tied behind her, a gag in her mouth, is Meghan.

I walk over, back straight, head in the air, mind on the fucking game.

Back to business.

Meghan is sat so her back is to me, but once I am in her sight, I see her face drop. She had to have known that this day would come. She couldn't get away with hiding in her brothers shadows forever.

"Meghan Morgan," I say as I stand in front of her, hands on my hips. Her eyes widen as I move towards her, making sure that we're eye level. "No need to look so worried, all I want to do is ask you some questions." It's my fake-as-hell voice talking, but there is no denying the underlying threat that laces my words.

"Take her gag off," I say to no one in particular, one of the boys will do it. And Donovan steps up, moving to the back of Meghan and gently undoing the knot to release the cloth that stops her from saying anything.

Donovan then stands back, his eyes still on Meghan.

Interesting again. His eyes are usually on me. Not that I mind, but I need him to be fully focussed for this to play out how I want.

"Don't you dare fucking touch her," Clive shouts from his cage. I turn around and glare at him.

"You are in no position to tell me what to do," I start. "And if you want her to come out of this alive, then I suggest you keep your fucking mouth shut."

"Bitch," I hear him mumble, but he settles down, leaning his back against the cage as he watches on.

Larry doesn't say a word. He looks defeated, like he knows his time is coming to an end far quicker than he would have liked.

I turn back to Meghan and she still has those wide eyes, along with a trembling bottom lip. I roll my eyes. As if a trembling lip and a woman on the verge of tears is about to stop me from forging ahead.

"So, Meghan, I guess you have already figured out why you are here?" I ask. I would rather know whether I am dealing with stupid or arrogant to begin with.

"Yes," she says quietly.

"Oh, come on, Meghan, speak up, your answers are going to need to be shared with the whole group," I say as I lift my arms to my sides, spreading them out so that she gets the idea of engaging with the whole fucking room.

She clears her throat. "Yes, I know why I'm here."

"Good—"

"It's because of those assholes," she says with a tilt of her head in her brother's direction. "They made me do it, I swear. I never wanted any part of it. I never wanted to be involved in anything they did," she rambles, giving me answers to questions that I never realised I wanted the answers to.

"They forced me to drive that car, they forced me to watch as they hurt Miles, they made me do it, I swear."

"Shut your fucking mouth," Clive shouts.

"No," she shouts back. "I've covered for you assholes for too long. I don't want this. I don't want to be associated with you," she says, almost spitting the last word out.

"Meghan, I swear, when I get out of here, shit is going to get bad for you real quick if you don't keep your fucking mouth shut," Clive continues, and I have heard enough of their family spat.

"Enough," I say loudly. "Clive, keep it shut or you will die within the next few seconds," I say as I raise my gun, click the safety off and point it in his direction.

"You're gonna fucking kill me anyway, so why drag it out?" he replies, trying to goad me.

"You know, I was just thinking the same thing," I say before I pull the trigger and fire. The sound of the bullet leaving the gun echoes around the room. It only takes a second for Clive's body to hit the ground, the thud ricocheting around us all.

"Well, that's one less pain in the ass to deal with," I say as I click the safety back on my gun and replace it in the back of my trousers. "You wanna be the next, Larry?"

He shakes his head, his eyes on his lifeless brother.

It wasn't the way I wanted to end Clive, I wanted him to suffer much more than just a bullet to the head, but he lived longer than he was supposed to, and at least now I don't have to deal with his incessant whining every time I come down here.

"Now, where were we?" I say, turning back to Meghan and her shocked-as-shit eyes. Surely, she isn't that surprised that this kind of stuff happens in this world? She has been the sister of the three biggest assholes to ever walk the earth, she must have seen plenty.

"Are you going to kill me?" she asks, her panicked eyes coming back to mine. Her eyes are quite pretty, being a turquoise colour, like two pools of clear blue sea. Her curly, black hair hangs around her face, albeit a little messy, but it could be styled nicely. And actually, she doesn't look like the brothers much; she's actually good-looking, unlike those assholes who look like they have just crawled out from under a rock.

"That depends… You going to give me the answers I need?" I ask her, lowering down to her level, making sure I have complete focus.

"Yes." No hesitation in her answer.

"Then we shouldn't have a problem, apart from the fact that you drove the car so that your brothers could stab my boy."

I feel Donovan's eyes flick to me. I give a slight nod of my head to confirm that Meghan was telling the truth when she said that she was driving the car. His nostrils flare, and I know that he would love nothing more than to beat the shit out of something right now just to get rid of some of his frustration. It's his lucky day because I'm letting him loose on Larry later. I have no need for the sad sack to be sticking around anymore. I have Meghan, and I am betting that she is going to give me all of the answers that I need.

"I didn't want to do it," she starts. "I didn't, I swear. I like Miles, and they won't even tell me if he is okay." I can see her eyes have worry lurking beneath them. Is she really worried about Miles? Or her life? This chick is going to take a little bit more figuring out.

"We'll talk about Miles later. Right now, I want to know where Bobby is," I say, standing to my full height again, crossing my arms in front of me.

"Don't do it, Meghan," Larry says, albeit a lot fucking quieter than his brother did.

I can hear the plea in his voice, Meghan can hear it too, but she's clearly had enough of her brothers to last a lifetime as she answers me.

"He's in the basement, underneath Morgan's." And there it is, the motherfucking jackpot answer.

"He been there all this time?" I ask, needing to know if there is anywhere else I should be looking.

"No. He was on a canal boat first, then when he got paranoid about being found, he took to the basement. He's been there ever since," she says like it's no big deal that she just gave up one of her own.

Very fucking interesting.

"Anyone else down there with him?"

"No. Just him. I take him food and drink, he shouts a load of abuse at me, and then I leave," she replies.

"Meghan, what have you done?" Larry says in disbelief.

"I've fucking ended it," she snaps back at him.

"You always were a stupid bitch," he spits. "Never good for anything."

"That's where you're wrong, dear brother," she says, the sarcasm dripping from her mouth. "I was never the stupid one. I watched, I waited, and now this is my fucking out. I never wanted to be associated with you. You might be related to me, but it's by blood only, and if I could change that fact then I would do it in a fucking heartbeat. I've always hated you, all of you. Making me work in your sleazy-ass restaurant, letting your friends cop a feel, making me drive for you and get involved in your shady shit. I'm done. And so are you."

Well.

Fucking bravo.

Nice little speech.

And definitely making me warm up to this chick, ever so slightly.

Maybe her being a woman has made her feel left out of her brothers' dealings. Maybe it's because she a hell of a lot younger than them. Or maybe it's because she genuinely doesn't share their disgusting thirst for life. Whatever it is, Meghan has fire, and I respect anyone with fire. Especially when they are packing a whole load of it, which she clearly is.

"Bray, Tony, you're staying here. Make sure that Meghan gets some food and a drink. Donovan, you're coming with me," I instruct. "And Larry," I say as I turn to face him with a sickly sweet smile on my face. "Countdown starts now, asshole. As soon as I bring Bobby's ass in here, the game is over, and then my boys get to have their fun."

I see him gulp, he does nothing to mask it as he sits next to his dead brother, the blood pooling from his head wound.

"Meghan, I'll deal with you later." It's the last thing I say before walking out, Donovan behind me, ready to go and kick some more ass.

Chapter Thirty Two
Joey

"Joey," Raymond says, walking into my office, the door flying open and hitting the wall. "We've got a problem."

"Another one?" I say, exasperated. Only a few hours ago I was in my bed, with my queen, and now I'm about to be bombarded with another issue to sort out.

"You're going to want to know about this one."

The edge to his voice has me looking away from my computer screen.

"I'm all ears," I say, gesturing for him to sit the fuck down. Raymond shuts the door and makes his way over, taking a seat, ready to give me the details of whatever it is I've got to deal with now.

"I've known you a long time, Joey, and I know that there is more to you and Paige than you're letting on, but it's your business and none of mine," he starts, and I lean back in my chair, waiting to see what his point is. "This is why I figured you would want to know that Bobby has Paige."

"Pardon?" I don't think I heard him correctly.

"Bobby fucking Morgan has got Paige."

"He can't have. She found him. She beat us to the punch," I say, fury starting to build inside of me.

"She didn't find him. She found his hiding spot, but he had already fled," Raymond informs me.

She didn't find him.

She lied.

He fled.

He's got her.

My Paige. My fucking queen.

"How do you know this?" I ask, because wherever he gets his intel from, I want in on it, and then I want to know why the fuck he's been keeping this source from me.

"Because Donovan is sat out front, his face busted up. He managed to get away, and he came straight here."

"He's fucking what?" I rage. "And he just left her with Bobby, on her fucking own?"

"Seems so, boss."

"Jesus fucking Christ," I fume before I stand up and march out of my office and out to the main room of the club.

He fucking left her.

Bastard.

As Donovan comes into view, he's slumped against the bar, a tumbler in his hand, his face dripping with blood. It'll be dripping with a hell of a lot more by the time I'm finished with him.

I storm over, fucking murder in my eyes. I don't even need to see my reflection to know that I look like the mean motherfucker that I am. The first thing I do is knock the tumbler out of Donovan's hand. The second thing is that I grab him by the scruff of his fucking neck, which I could so easily break right about now. And third, I ask, "Where the fuck is she?"

"Under Morgan's restaurant, in the basement," Donovan answers, looking every bit as defeated as he should feel.

"Raymond, Nate, Pascal, Big Danny, you're coming with me. Gary, Leon and Simon, you make sure this asshole doesn't go anywhere," I say, pointing at Donovan. "I'll deal with you later."

I leave the threat hanging in the air and stalk out of the club before another word can be spoken and get in my car.

Raymond gets in the passenger seat, and the boys get in the car behind. They all know to give me a bit of fucking breathing room right now.

I start the car and then we're off, flying in the direction of the Morgan restaurant.

"I have to ask, Joey, is this shit real, are we doing this because she's one of us?" Raymond asks me, needing to know how far I will go for this woman and whether I expect my boys to put their necks on the line.

It doesn't matter that she lied right now. I'm pissed about it, but that happened before we reclaimed one another.

It doesn't matter that I'm meant to be putting on a fucking show for the rest of the underworld.

What matters is that I need to go get my queen, and I expect my men to go down trying if that is what it takes.

"She's one of us," I confirm, and I floor the accelerator, making the car go faster.

She's always been one of us.

Chapter Thirty Three
Paige

Well done, Paige. Go after Bobby with just Donovan and end up becoming the fucking target.

Bobby had done his homework. He knew that I wouldn't see him as much of a threat on his own. How very, very stupid of me. It's the first time in a long time that my danger instincts have been way off. Idiot, idiot, idiot.

He's clearly been watching my moves from the start. But how? Someone must have been helping him, and when I get out of this mess, I will make it my personal mission to find out who. And they will wish that they had never crossed me.

I don't think I have ever been this furious in my entire life.

Brought to my knees by a fucking Morgan. Ugh.

I'm currently holed up in the basement underneath Morgan's, tied to a fucking chair, just like Meghan was tied up back at my place. Bobby is stood across the room from me, watching me like I'm his prey. He better believe I'm going to rain down a world of shit on him when I get out of these ties.

I've been prepared for this.

I've had Donovan tie me to a chair more than once, just to see make sure that I can get out of any situation.

I'm taking my time, making sure that Bobby doesn't twig what I'm up to.

Slowly moving my wrists, wiggling my fingers, trying to get the damn pocket knife that is hidden beneath my long sleeved top to move the fuck down, so I can cut myself free from this bullshit situation.

Donovan and I were ambushed from the off. Three guys waiting to take out Donovan, and Bobby waiting to take me out.

Donovan. Donovan fucking Marshall. He got away, and he left me here. He escaped without even thinking about taking me with him. He knows I'm not some damsel in distress, he knows that I can take care of myself, but abandoning me? There is no coming back from that.

Total trust, his words. We've always had it, apart from speaking about Joey. And my reasons for that are justified. My love life has fuck all to do with the business that goes down, and Donovan knowing about my past is of no relevance to how we conduct ourselves. He may be pissed, but this is the shittiest way of showing it. Leaving your queen to the wolves. Bastard.

It's quite apparent that I am no longer his queen. He is no longer my right hand man. And I have no idea how to process that right now. He's been with me since day one, and for it to end like this is a total blow to my mind.

If Donovan has gone into hiding, it better be in a fucking good place because I will search for him for all of eternity.

"So, Paige Roderick, or should I say, Daniels?" Bobby says, a smirk on his ugly-ass face. "Imagine my surprise when I stumbled across some information that gave me a wealth of knowledge about your past." He pulls a notebook out of his trouser pocket and flips it open.

"Yes, here it is… Started out as nothing, came from the gutter, wanted revenge, used to be in love with Joey Valentine, made it a personal mission to take him down and make sure to be top of the chain. Have I missed anything out?" He chuckles. "I gotta tell you, Paige, when you showed up to confront my stupid-ass brothers, I thought that you would have done your homework properly, found out whether all three of us would have been there, but it seems that even the great Joey Valentine couldn't help you out on that one."

His laughter is pissing me off, and I keep working to get the damn knife to my hand, so I can start to cut away at the rope tying me to this goddamn chair.

"I guess there's no harm in telling you who gave me this delicious intel," he says, and I feign ignorance even though I am dying to know who it was.

"Seems your crew aren't as tight as you think. You and your boys, thinking they run the fucking playing field when all you have been is a part of my plan.

"Everyone thought that Larry was the brains behind the Morgan brothers, but they couldn't have been further from the truth. I've stayed hidden, acted the fucking dumbass, but I always ran the show. Me. No one else. They were nothing but my minions that played out the scenes, gave me the answers and the room to grow."

Motherfucker.

"You know, Paige, seeing you here, tied up, waiting on my next move, it's something of a turn on," he says whilst grabbing his dick with his hand and acting an even bigger asshole than usual. Thank God his trousers are zipped up because if he pulled that thing out then I may actually puke.

I manage to shimmy the knife down and bingo, it's in my hand and I get to work, slowly starting to cut the rope. It's going to take me a hot minute, but I'll do it, I have no doubt at my ability to get the fuck out of this scenario.

And I certainly don't need a man to come and save my ass. That ship sailed a long time ago.

"I have to admit that I never expected Donovan to bail. Thought you two were tight, best buds, actually thought you were both fucking one another at one point. But then the info about Joey landed in my lap, and I knew that you couldn't be fucking Donovan." He continues to prattle on and I continue to cut.

"I must give my upmost thanks to Tony for telling me everything that I needed to know."

Tony.

Fucking Tony is my mole?

I'll kill him.

"He sure does know how to slither like a snake amongst the powerful. He's been giving me intel for months. What's your number one rule, Paige? Trust nobody, that's it. Fucking stupid female." He doubles over laughing and that is when my wrists break free. I poke the knife back up my sleeve and wait.

Bobby sure does like the sound of his own voice.

"Here's how this is going to play out. I'm going to take my time with you, touch you, lick you, taste you. You're going to scream, I'm going to love the sound, and then I'm going to gut you like a fucking fish," he says as he stalks towards me, bending down so that he's eye level as he comes to a stop right in front of me.

The putrid smell of his sweat hits my nostrils and I fight hard to not screw my nose up from the aroma.

I let a smile grace my lips.

He's so not going to be prepared for what I am about to do.

"You know, Bobby, you really should cover all angles before you tie a woman up and threaten her."

"I did cover all angles," he insists, his nostrils flaring.

"You sure about that?" I say, tilting my head to the side in question. "You see, most men tend to underestimate me, and that is the biggest mistake that they make."

"I haven't underestimated you, bitch. You're no longer running things around here, I am. I am the top fucking dog, and once I've gutted you, I'm going after Joey," he shouts as if he is trying to convince himself more than anything else.

Now it's my turn to laugh.

"You think you're going to get to Joey?"

"I got to you, I can get to him."

"I always thought you were stupid, Bobby, but not delusional," I reply.

His hand flies out and slaps me across my face. My head swings to the side from the blow, but I block out the pain. I can deal with that later. Right now I need to stay on my game. My head quickly turns back to him, and just when he is about to rain another blow down on me, I pounce.

A swift kick to the nuts and a punch to the jaw.

Bobby's knees buckle, and he goes down howling. Stupid fucker thought he could overpower me. Now he's about to learn.

As he goes to get back up, I slam my knee into his jaw, sending him flying backwards. He's down and I'm not about to let him get back up. I move over him, punch after punch hitting his smug-ass face.

His hands fly out, hitting at my sides, his legs kicking out, trying to get me off of him, but once I go, I'm like a fucking force field. I may only be a petite woman, but I pack a goddamn punch and then some.

Minutes pass by and still he fights against me, but I can see he's getting tired. Built for speed? More like built to be a sloth.

His nose is pouring out blood, his hands are still jabbing at my sides, and I'm still not finished. I pull the pocket knife out of my sleeve and let the glint of the steel catch his eye.

"Oh no you don't, bit—"

He doesn't get to say another word as I plunge the knife into his throat and gargling noises take over.

I hold the knife there, watching the life drain out him.

"You never had a chance of running the fucking game, Bobby, and now you never will," I say, disgust lacing my tone.

His arms go limp, falling to the floor, his legs stop kicking, but I don't move an inch until I watch him take his last breath.

I took down one of the biggest assholes to walk the streets.

On my own.

But I feel no relief. I feel no elation.

All I feel is hurt. Hurt by Donovan and hurt by Tony.

Maybe this world is no longer for me?

Maybe I've done my time and now is when I get the fuck out.

Trust. It's something that isn't easily earned and can never be repaired.

Two of my boys have broken that.

Two of my own.

And I have no idea how I am going to get over it.

Chapter Thirty Four
Joey

Fucking hell, these assholes needs to move the hell out of my way.

The three ogres blocking the door to Morgan's are about to die. I need to get in there, see if my girl is okay. I know she can handle herself, but I'm still a man who would die to protect his own.

I move forwards, in plain sight, pull my gun and shoot. Goon number one drops, then two, then three. I step over the bodies as if it's just another day at the office, which for me, it is.

This lifestyle isn't for everyone, hell, it isn't totally for me anymore, but I'll always be in it, as long as Paige is. Wherever she goes, I will follow. Doesn't make me a lapdog, it makes me a man that is totally in love with a fucking queen who deserves nothing but the best.

I'm that for her. Me.

There is a strong possibility that she may kick my ass after all of this, because she won't want to be rescued, as she puts it, but I don't care. I'll let her kick my ass, and I'll enjoy every goddamn minute of it.

"Get rid of them," I bark as I step over the dead goons and push the door to the restaurant open.

I enter and there is silence.

Nothing.

I move to where I know the basement is located by the sheer fact that the trap door is wide open.

I pause and listen again. Nothing.

Shit. This isn't good.

My heart beats wildly and I start to take the steps down.

I swear to God, if he's killed her, I'll maul him to death with my bare hands.

But, as I get to the bottom step and look around, I guess I won't have to maul him, because he's already dead, bleeding out on the concrete floor.

And there is Paige, led beside him, eyes closed, and the sheer panic hits me full force.

I race over, forgetting to check to see if any other fucker is down here waiting to take me out.

My only thoughts are Paige and if she is breathing.

I place my fingers on her neck, feeling for a pulse, and I breathe a sigh of relief that there is one.

I run my eyes over her and notice that her top has ridden up a bit, showing angry red marks on her skin.

Marks that will leave bruises, and possibly reminders of whatever the fuck she went through down here, alone, with no one stood beside her.

"Joey," Raymond says from behind me. "The boys are moving the bodies now. I'll get this asshole taken care of, you take care of Paige."

As if I wasn't going to do that anyway.

I gently slide my arms beneath her, a little bit fucking scared to move her in case I cause any more damage to her body, but I can't leave her here, and I sure as shit won't let anyone else put their hands on her. I lift her up and hold her against my body. She doesn't move, totally passed out from whatever went on.

I nod to Raymond as I leave and make my way out of the restaurant and back to my car. I lie her on the back seat, wishing I could hold her against me, but knowing full well I have to get out of here and let my boys get to work on cleaning this place up and disposing of the bodies.

I get in the driver's seat and start the engine. It roars to life, and then we're off.

Back to my place.
Back to safety.
And far away from all things Morgan related.

Chapter Thirty Five
Paige

My eyes fly open and I jolt upright, only to wish that I hadn't as pain radiates through my entire body. I let out a groan and close my eyes for a second, breathing in and out, trying to reduce the fucking searing that is shooting through my body.

Christ. Bobby did a fucking number on me. He may be dead, but I'm going to remember this pain forever. I've never been this badly injured physically, ever.

Opening my eyes again, I let them look around the room. A room that isn't mine. A room that I didn't expect to be in. Joey Valentine's bedroom, and I'm in his bed.

"How the fuck did I get here?" I say to no one seeing as I'm the only one in here. The last thing I remember is stabbing Bobby in the neck and watching the life drain out of him.

I try to rack my brains for some hint of how I got here, but I come up clueless.

I need to get out of here. I need to go back home and give Donovan and Tony a piece of my mind, the two-faced bastards.

I struggle to get myself to the edge of the bed, grunting with every movement. This shit hurts. So much for coming out of it a fucking warrior. I'm a goddamn mess.

"What the fuck do you think you are doing?" I hear from behind me, and I jump, making the pain fire through me once again.

"Ah, motherfucker," I say as I grit my teeth.

"Shit, Paige," Joey says as he stands in front of me. "You need to rest."

"No, I need to get out of here and go take care of business," I tell him, although there is no confidence in my voice, the energy it has taken to move myself has drained me.

Joey easily lifts my legs back into the bed and covers me over with the duvet.

"Joey, I seriously have stuff to do," I tell him.

He just looks at me as if I have gone insane. "You have nothing to do but lie your ass in that bed and let me take care of you."

"I can't just stay in here," I argue. "I have shit to run."

"Not at the moment you don't." He's not budging, but then I'm not exactly a fucking walkover, so I'm not about to give up.

"Joey, listen to me, you know that I can't just take time off. You know that I have things to deal with, so you know that I need to leave this goddamn room."

"Paige, I love your determination, your fire and the sexy independent woman thing you got going on, but for the love of God, if you don't listen to me on this, I will tie you to the fucking bed." He's serious. Completely and utterly serious.

"I can get out of ties," I respond sassily. I did it not too long ago, and I could do it again.

"Then I'll handcuff you," he says, a slight smile pulling at his lips.

"I can pick a lock."

"Then I'll use fucking cable ties, hell, I'll even tighten the damn things so there is no wiggle room." Yeah, he's not backing down, and for the first time in a long time, I don't think I'm going to get my own way here.

"You gonna cater to my every need, big guy?"

"Every single fucking second of the day," he replies, no hesitation.

I let a soft smile grace my lips at his answer. This is the side of Joey that turns me on like no other. Raw, powerful, determined. Nothing is sexier.

"This could be fun," I say, and he lets out a low chuckle.

"I have no doubt that you will have me doing shit that I never ever dreamt I would do," he replies as he lowers himself down so he's sitting on the edge of the bed, facing me.

"Well, it wouldn't be very entertaining if I didn't."

"I look forward to the challenge," he says, and then he leans in for a kiss. A soft, toe-curling, panty-melting kiss.

He rests his forehead against mine, and I swear, it is the most heart-warming moment. I don't have them often anymore, but fuck, I could get used to feeling like this around Joey. It's not hard to slip back into old ways and old feelings. I just have to make sure that I don't get lost in the process.

"What happened, Joey?" I ask. "How come I ended up in your bed?"

He lets out a sigh. "Donovan came to me after he got away from those fucking goons. He said that Bobby had you."

"And you came to find me?"

"Nothing in the fucking world would have stopped me, Paige," he says, his eyes boring into mine as he moves his head back slightly. "I know you can handle your own shit, but I have never been as fucking scared as I was in that moment."

"Scared?" I whisper, his truth shocking me.

"Yes, Paige, scared. I lost you once before, and I don't plan on losing you ever again."

Oh my God.

All of those girly feelings bubble up within me, like they used to, and I do nothing to stop them.

"But we've only just..." My voice fades off as I try to find the words I want to speak.

"Only just what? Only just made up? Only just started figuring our shit out?" Joey finishes for me and I nod my head in response.

"Who cares how long we've been figuring it out?" he continues. "Who says that there is a time limit on what we fucking do? It's not like we've only just met, Paige. We've known each other for years. We've argued, we've ignored one another, we've been cut-throat, but none of that fucking matters. All that matters is that we are here, together, and I'll fight any bastard that tries to come between us.

"I was an idiot all those years ago, and I'm not about to make the same mistakes again. I know my truth, Paige, but the question here is, do you know yours?"

His words, his questions, it's all so much.

I've spent years hiding the old me beneath layers of Paige Roderick, and he's made his way through them all, without even trying, because he was always there. Beneath the surface. Holding my heart. Consuming my soul.

It's always been Joey.

I've been fooling myself for years.

I either give up the fight and give myself to him fully, or I walk away.

Walk away. It's no longer an option.

I'm about to bring a part of Paige Daniels back.

She's not weak, she's just a girl in love with a badass man.

She's a girl who never got her chance the first time around.

And she's a girl I will no longer be ashamed of.

I may have moulded myself into a queen of the underworld, but beneath it all, I'm still the woman that wants to be loved by the guy of her dreams.

I don't have to give up the new me, and I don't have to give up the old.

I can be both.

They're the same person.

They're both me.

A girl in love with a boy. A woman in love with a man.

Paige Daniels and Paige Roderick. Same person, same heart, and totally in love with the man in front of her.

Joey Valentine.

My kryptonite.

He looks at me with all that hope in his eyes, and it soothes me, makes me wonder why the hell I kept fighting for so long.

Second chances aren't always given, but we deserve ours.

My mouth opens, and I speak the words that I never thought I would again.

"I love you, big guy. I never stopped."

Chapter Thirty Six
Joey

"I love you, big guy. I never stopped."

Those words.

Fuck.

I've been waiting to hear them for so damn long.

Music to my ears.

Warmth to my cold-blooded heart.

Fire in my veins.

My queen.

My love.

My whole fucking heart.

Paige Daniels, the one that got away, the one that came back, and the one that I am going to worship every goddamn day.

She's my ride or die.

A smile breaks across my face and I cup her face in my hands.

"I fucking love you too, Paige. Always have, and I'll never, ever stop," I tell her, meaning every single word more than I ever have before.

"You going all mushy on me, Joey?" she teases.

"Fuck yes." And then I connect my lips with her, tasting her, devouring her, claiming her all over again. And it feels oh-so-fucking good.

This is where I'm meant to be.

This is where we should have been all along.

Together. Unbreakable. King and queen. Side by side. Equals in everything.

And I am so ready to show the whole damn underworld that we are the motherfucking force that will rule together.

Chapter Thirty Seven
Paige

It's been a few days since the ordeal with Bobby, and I'm feeling better physically. The marks have turned into bruises, and the pain is subsiding with each day that passes.

I haven't returned to my house yet as Joey has been adamant about holing me up in his bedroom and waiting until I was able to move about more freely. I would love to say that he has been fucking me senseless, but he has refrained, didn't want to make the pain I was experiencing any worse. He's got the restraint of a motherfucking celibate in a whore house.

I told him all about Tony's shady antics, had to stop him going over there and putting a bullet in the bastard's head. Also had to stop him from kicking Donovan's ass. Those boys are mine to deal with how I see fit, and that's what I'm doing now, making my way to the front door of my home, ready to confront the bastards that played me and left me behind.

I have my head held high, ready to get back to business, and I have Joey behind me.

You see, what the others don't know yet is that we are joining forces.

Putting our gangs together.

Becoming the ultimate fucking leaders.

Joey and I told his boys this morning, and I'm telling mine now. Well, I'm informing the snakes to make them run scared, and then I'm telling the rest of my boys that they can join us for the ride.

As I walk through the front door, there stands Bray, guarding it like he always does. I'm pretty sure he's still a good boy that does as he's told.

189

"Bray," I greet him, and he nods his head at me.

"How are you doing, boss?" he asks.

"I'm good. Where's Donovan?"

"Down in the basement keeping Meghan company."

"Is he now? Been down there a lot, has he?" I enquire.

"Everyday."

At one time this interested me, but now, now I couldn't give a shit. He's going to be out on his ass in the next few minutes and then he can find someone else to go and betray.

"Tony down there too?"

"Yes, boss," Bray tells me.

"How's Miles doing?"

"Nearly all better. The doctor checks in twice a day, but he'll be ready to do the running again in a few days."

"Excellent," I reply.

"And where's Rome?"

"Out back, keeping watch."

"Trevor and Grace still here?"

"Yes, boss. They won't leave until you give them the go ahead."

Seems my boy Bray knows it all, and he's quickly looking like he might just be my next right hand man.

"Thanks, Bray. You keep guard. Joey and I will be in the basement if you need either of us."

"Sure thing," he says, and I start to walk to the basement, Joey following me. I'll fill Bray in on what's happening later. Right now, I'm focussed on Donovan and Tony, and getting them the fuck out of here.

Joey doesn't say a word as he follows me into the basement. He's been prepped on how this is going to play out.

"Gentleman," I say as I finish descending the stairs and walk towards Donovan and Tony, who are stood at the end of the room, Meghan sat to the side, eating a bowl of something. She stops what she is doing, as do the boys, and all of their eyes go wide at my unannounced arrival.

"Paige," Donovan says before his eyes slide to Joey who is stood right behind me, almost touching me, his chest to my back.

"Hey, boss," Tony says nervously. "Where have you been?"

His fucking pathetic attempt to act clueless has me scoffing.

"Why don't you take a seat, boys," I say as Joey goes to the side of the room and brings two chairs either side of me before resuming his God-like stance.

I can't wait to get beneath him later. It's been a fucking struggle being around him, sleeping in his bed and him not giving it up.

"Come on, boys, don't keep me waiting," I say as I cross my arms and tap my foot, waiting for them to take a seat. Meghan has dropped her spoon, her food forgotten as she watches on. I'll deal with her a little later. She's not off of my shit list.

"That's right," I say condescendingly as they take their seats.

Joey stands behind them, and I stand in front, facing them, working up to tearing them a new asshole.

"So, how's things been running whilst I've been away?" I ask, waiting to see who will answer me first. It would usually be Donovan, but I'm betting Tony is so fucking nervous right now that he will be the first to speak up.

"It's been good, boss. All running smoothly," Tony says. Bingo. Fucking fool. Even Donovan's face pulls into a frown.

"Is that so?"

"Sure," he replies, shrugging his shoulders.

"Well, I gotta say, I'm a little shocked," I start, dragging it out, making them wait.

"About what, boss?" Tony asks, pretending to be the clueless prick.

"You know, I've always run a tight ship, expected the best results, always paid handsomely."

"We know that, boss," Tony says, and his ass-kissing is starting to really irritate me.

"I always looked after my boys, would go to war for them. But, the last few days have shown me that my rules have been disrespected more than once.

"Loyalty between each other. It's the fucking core of our relationships, and a dirty, slimy, snake is skulking among us."

Out of the corner of my eye I see Tony gulp, whilst Donovan's eyes remain locked on mine.

"You know what I do to snakes that slither about and think that they have been undetected?" I ask, even though they both know exactly how I deal with those types of assholes.

"Whose ass we gotta go and kick?" Tony asks me. The fucking nerve of him. He's still trying to cover his God damn tracks? Total idiot. I see Joey's nostrils flare, but his time will come. I have my fun first, Joey gets his second.

Don't worry, big guy, this asshole is all yours in a few minutes. My gift to you, baby.

I let out a short laugh before walking over to Tony and leaning down, so I'm eye level with the fucker. I want to see every bit of goddamn uncertainty in his eyes as I tell him what his fate is going to be.

"I don't think you can kick your own ass, Tony."

His mouth opens and shuts several times, but he has no words. He knows his time is up.

"You sealed your fucking fate the moment that you gave intel to Bobby Morgan."

I hear Donovan gasp and Tony gulp.

"You gave him what he needed to know to come after me, after all of us. You betrayed me, and that never goes unpunished."

"I'm sorry, boss—"

"You don't get to call me that anymore. I'm not your boss, and I never will be again."

He wisely shuts his mouth, waiting for the next part.

"You fed me to the wolves, Tony, and now I'm going to do the same to you."

His eyes widen, and I stand tall, ready to deliver my final blow.

"You wanna finish this off, big guy?" I say to Joey and the look on Tony and Donovan's face is fucking priceless. Joey smirks and walks round to stand beside me, his arm going around my waist, leaving no room for mistake on what is happening here.

"Not only did you fuck with Paige, but you fucked with me by going against her. Bad fucking move," Joey starts and the venom in his voice has me wanting to rip his clothes off of him.

"No one, and I mean no one, goes against my queen and gets away with it."

Fuck me.

His queen.

Badass Joey Valentine showing them what I mean to him. Damn. He's gonna get the blow job of a lifetime later on. I'll make sure to blow his mind like he's blowing mine right now.

"Joey... Please... I didn't—"

"Don't fucking beg like a dog," Joey says, cutting Tony off. "I have no interest in your pathetic excuses. All I'm interested in is feeding you to those wolves, and taking a few shots myself," Joey says, and I know that he will enjoy giving this fucker hell.

"My boys are out the front, ready and waiting, so move your ass and don't make me tell you again," he says to Tony, and Tony is instantly on his feet.

"I'll see you later, baby," he says before planting a kiss on my lips and rocking my world a little bit more.

He breaks away and follows Tony, pushing him to hurry the fuck up. I told him I wanted to speak to Donovan on my own. I know Meghan is here with us, but I'm not worried about her witnessing this. I just didn't want Joey in here to see how much hurt Donovan has caused me, because if he did, then he would probably bury the bastard before I had the chance to finish what I need to say.

I look to Donovan and he looks sad. He knows he's next in the firing line, but he doesn't know what path his life is going to take just yet. I'm the one that gets to decide that, and I know what I have to do.

"We've been in this together for a long time, Donovan, so I would appreciate not being lied to right now," I start. "I get why you wanted to escape, to run, to save yourself, but to leave me behind? After everything we have been through?" I can't help but show how much his betrayal has affected me.

"I'm sorry, Paige, you will never know how sorry, but I knew I couldn't take them on alone. I knew we needed help, and that's why I went to Joey."

"We never had Joey before all of this, Don. We only ever had us. What happened? What changed?" I ask, needing to know.

"Christ, Paige. I will never forgive myself for leaving, ever. I already know that things are broken between us, I see it in your eyes, I feel it in here," he says, putting his hand over his heart. "I just knew that I wasn't what you needed any longer. You needed Joey, and I went to get him."

"Bobby could have fucking killed me, Don."

"He wouldn't have killed you. You were always too smart for the men in this world. I knew you would be okay, I knew you could handle yourself. It's what we had always trained for, to make sure we survived in the deadliest situation."

"You had no idea that I would come out of this alive," I argue. No one could have known that. I mean, I'm flattered that he had so much faith in me, but it could have gone down differently, and I wouldn't be standing here today if it had.

"Paige, you know you're a strong fucking woman. You know that you can deal with anything. I never doubted you, not even for a second. I went to get Joey because I knew that you would want him there over everybody else. I saw it between you both from the off. I knew that things were going to change, but fuck, I didn't realise they were going to change so quickly," he says.

"I wanted to believe that it was just me seeing things that weren't there, me reading too much into it, but I wasn't. And I know that I will never match up to Joey Valentine."

What the fuck is he saying right now?

My confusion must be evident on my face because he answers without me even asking a question.

"I'm in love with you, Paige. Have been since the first moment I laid eyes on you," he says, and knock me over with a feather, I was not expecting that. All this time, and I never knew, never even had an inkling. Before all of this went down, I thought he had the hots for Meghan with the way he was eye-balling her when she was brought in here. Jesus.

"I know that my place in your world no longer exists, but just know that if he ever, ever fucking hurts you, I will come and kick his sorry ass all over the damn place," Donovan says and in the midst of all this truth, I fucking laugh. Highly inappropriate for the topic, but the idea of him kicking Joey's ass tickles me.

Donovan allows himself a smile. "I'm sorry it ended like this, Paige." He sounds just as sad as his eyes look and I can't help but soften a little. We've been through so much together. This moment is final. It's how we say goodbye, and it's where I forgive Donovan for his faux pas and move on. He doesn't deserve to die today. He knows he fucked up, and that's enough.

"Me too, Don."

"Good luck to the underworld, they're going to need it with you two running the show," he says, and there is no malice in his words. He means them, and I agree. They're all going to need the best of luck to deal with the force coming their way.

I smile, he smiles, and then he's gone, walking away and out of my life for good. No hugs, no peck on the cheek, that's not how we do things around here. Joey wanted to slit Donovan's throat for leaving me with Bobby, I had to demand that he left Donovan to me, and I'm glad that I did because Donovan isn't a bad guy, he just made a shitty decision that cost him his job, and ultimately, our bond.

"Damn, lady, you gotta teach me how you handle all of these men," Meghan says, looking at me like I'm a fucking enigma.

I can't help but laugh.

It takes time, but maybe I'll teach her a few tricks. All she has to do is convince me that she really did hate her brothers as much as I did, and I'm pretty sure I already know the answer to that, even if my gut intuition has been a little bit off lately.

Chapter Thirty Eight
Joey

Is there any better sight than the woman you love bent over, her head bobbing up and down on your dick?

Nope, there isn't, and fuck if I am not about to explode in her mouth.

I let out a deep growl as she twirls her tongue, slowly, deliciously, and fucking torturously.

Woman of my dreams, taking what she wants.

I'm a lucky bastard.

She sucks harder, and I'm done, a loud roar erupting and my dick unloading in her mouth. Jesus fucking Christ.

She lifts her head and winks at me before climbing up my body and straddling me. Oh yeah, fucking perfect.

"Better, big guy?" she purrs whilst running her fingernails lightly up and down my chest.

"You have no idea," I say, feeling all kinds of relaxed.

Her hands move to the bottom of her vest top, and she pulls it up slowly, until she is throwing it on the floor, along with her bra, revealing herself to me.

She's perfect. Perfect for me, perfect full fucking stop.

My eyes roam over her body, but they stop on the bruises that cover her skin.

I swear to God, I could dig Bobby's body up and kill him all over again.

Asshole.

"Hey," she says softly, taking my eyes back to hers. "They're just bruises, they don't hurt, and they won't be there forever."

I trace my fingers over them. "I still don't like seeing them. He hurt you, and that makes me feel fucking dangerous." No one touches her. No one hurts her. No fucking one.

"He's gone, we're here, and right now, I'm all yours," she says and before she knows what is happening, I flip her on her back, caging her in, covering her with my body.

"You're always mine," I growl, nuzzling her neck.

"So protective," she whispers.

"Is that a problem?"

"Not at all, Valentine," she answers because succumbing to moans of approval of me nibbling her ear lobe. "You know that if any other woman puts her hands on you, I'm gonna take them out, make them suffer, show them who you belong to."

"Ditto, baby, fucking ditto."

"You're gonna show women not to touch me?" she teases.

"You know what I mean, smartass," I reply before moving down and licking her nipple.

She arches her back, pushing into me, and my fingers find their way to her pussy. Her already wet pussy.

"No other man would get near you, Paige. You don't want to know what would happen if they laid their hands on you," I say, but the threat of my words doesn't deter her playfulness.

"Maybe I do wanna know."

"Well, if any fucker tries it, I'll be sure to give you a front row seat," I say before I swoop down and eat that pussy of hers that I love so much.

I could die and go to heaven right now and I wouldn't have a damn complaint.

I've had a fantastic day. Kicked some ass, took out another asshole, had my queen suck my cock like it was the last thing she was ever going to do, buried my face in the woman of my dreams, and then I get to make love to her, over and over again.

Yeah, it's a fucking great time to be Joey Valentine.

Chapter Thirty Nine
Paige

Forty-eight hours sure can change the course of your life.

One minute you think you're running the show, and then the next, you're on your way to share it with someone else.

Forty-eight hours ago, Joey and I decided our next steps.

Forty-seven hours ago he was fucking me senseless, reminding me of the pleasure he brings to my mind and body.

Thirty-eight hours ago, I told my remaining boys that my house was no longer my headquarters. They are going to be staying there, but my actual base will now be at Joey's place or, should I say, ours. Joey didn't want to waste another moment, and I couldn't have agreed more. So, I moved in, and we are both running our operations from there.

Thirty-seven hours ago, Miles went back to work, and Trevor and Grace went back to their place. They're safe now that all of the Morgan boys are out of the picture.

Thirty-six hours ago, I escorted all of my clothes and personal belongings to our place, to which Joey exclaimed that I had a lot of crap, I told him to bite me, he did, and then he screwed my brains out.

Thirty hours ago, we got out of bed, I put my things in their new place, we ate some food, and then we decided to fuck some more. Couldn't think of anything else I would rather have done.

Twenty-six hours ago, I finally asked Meghan everything that I needed to. She complied, she seemed to answer honestly, she showed no emotions towards her brothers other than disgust, and she asked if she could become part of my world. I thought about it, chewed it over, spoke to Joey because we're a fucking team, and we decided to give her shot, see what she was made of. We've got eyes on her at all times, just until we are satisfied that she can be truly trusted.

Twenty-four hours ago, Joey asked me how I knew that he wanted out of the underworld. I told him that it was a lucky guess and I was calling his bluff, asked him if he still wanted out, to which he said that he would stand beside me in this crazy fucked-up world for as long as I wanted to remain a part of it. Wherever I go, he goes, and vice versa.

Twelve hours ago, I went shopping. I needed something new to wear for tonight, for when I walk into Joey's club, with my entourage behind me, ready to blow the lid off of our union.

Two hours ago, I kicked Joey out of the house, made him go to the club ahead of me, didn't want him to see what I had bought.

One hour ago, I finished getting ready.

Thirty minutes ago, I surveyed myself in the mirror one last time before being convinced that this look was going to blow Joey mind and have his dick harder than rock. I know that my man is a fan of all things leather on me, namely my leather clad ass. So, to honour that, I bought a skin tight leather skirt, falls just above the knees, has a little slit going up my leg. I paired that with a black, lace body con, shows some flesh but not too much. It's long-sleeved and it will have Joey counting down the minutes until he can rip it off of me. Leather and lace; dude doesn't stand a chance.

I put on bright red lipstick, paired it with smoky eyes, and put on my killer stilettos, whilst leaving my long blond hair down and making it wild with curls. Mamma's ready to go play.

Ten minutes ago I pulled up outside of Club Valentine to see my boys and Meghan waiting for me. Grace isn't here tonight because she's heavily pregnant and a club is not the place for a lady who is about to pop. Trevor is here though, he showed up for the both of them.

Seven minutes ago I made my way over to them, only for Meghan to screech about how insanely hot I look. Got to say, it cemented my decision on all things leather and lace.

One minute ago, I walked through the doors of Club Valentine, flanked by my crew.

And now I stand, at the edge of the dance floor, seeing that the whole underworld elite are already here, drinking their choice of liquor, their fake-ass mistresses on their knees, and their big words meaning fuck all when it really comes down to it.

They're all about to get a lesson in who they will answer to from now on. Makes me smile, and what makes that smile even wider is the man waiting on the other side of the dance floor for me. Joey fucking Valentine.

He's stood there in black suit trousers, black dress shoes, white shirt that has the top couple of buttons undone and the sleeves rolled up to his elbows. His hair is a little messy, his stubble making him look all kinds of rugged. Christ, it doesn't get more divine than that.

My heart is already fluttering from seeing him, his hands in his pockets, his eyes trained on me. They roam up and down my body, and they ignite, showing me the fire that he holds inside for me.

I smirk.

Oh yeah, this is exactly how my life was meant to play out.

I may have had my heart broken by him long ago, but I know that he isn't going to do it again.

I'm his world, and he is now mine.

As it always should have been.

A second chance, and an even deadlier flame than before. A flame that will burn for all of eternity, and there isn't anything that will put it out.

The beat of the music throbs through the club, the bass vibrating all around.

Joey starts to walk towards me, and people start to watch him as he comes for me.

Bring it on, baby. I'm ready to show them what we're all about.

With each step he takes my sex tingles in anticipation of him touching me.

What that man can do with his hands is nobody's business but mine, and I smile at the thought.

He stops in front of me and I place my hands on my hips.

"You ready to throw down, baby?"

He smirks, and I grin.

He doesn't answer but reaches for my hands and pulls me onto the dance floor.

I can feel everyone's eyes on us.

Time stops.

The music pounds, and he takes me in his arms and starts to move.

"Let's give them all the show that they didn't know they needed," he says in my ear.

Yes, let's show them.

Paige Roderick and Joey Valentine.

A woman and a man who eventually found their way back to each other.

Chapter Forty
Joey

This woman.

She fucking slays me.

One look at her in that leather and lace get up and I couldn't stay away any longer.

I had to touch her, hold her, show them all that she is fucking mine.

When you let something go and then it comes back to you, you don't take that for granted.

I'm Joey Valentine, and she is my kryptonite, and I'm going to enjoy every single fucking moment of her working her way beneath my skin.

She will challenge me.

She will champion me.

She gave me her heart.

She gave me her love.

She gave me a second chance.

We stand together. United.

She's it for me.

And as we dance in front of all the assholes of the underworld, I know that she will one day dance in my arms as my wife, and I can't fucking wait.

The music dies down and she places her lips beside my ear.

"Checkmate, big guy."

Best checkmate of my fucking life.

The End.

To keep up to date with book news, you can find Lindsey on social media:
Facebook:
www.facebook.com/lindseypowellperfect
Twitter:
www.twitter.com/Lindsey_perfect
Instagram:
www.instagram.com/lindseypowellperfect
Goodreads: www.goodreads.com/lpow21
You can also follow her at her amazon author page:
www.amazon.com/author/lindseypowell

And you can also check out Lindsey's website where you can find all of her books, read her book review blog, and check out her Wattpad stories:
https://lindseypowellauthor.wordpress.com

About the Author

Lindsey lives in South West, England, with her partner and two children. She works within a family run business, and she began her writing career in 2013. She finds the time to write in-between working and raising a family.

Book series by Lindsey:
The Perfect Series: Perfect Stranger, Perfect Memories, Perfect Disaster, Perfect Beginnings
Part of Me Series: Part of Me, Part of You, Part of Us

Other books written by Lindsey:
Fixation (psychological thriller)
Take Me (romantic suspense)

Lindsey's love of reading inspired her to create her own book series. Her favourite book genre is romance, but her interests span over several genre's including mystery, suspense and crime.

Author Acknowledgments

First of all, I would like to say thank you for reading Paige and Joey's story.

For my tenth book, I wanted something extra special, and I got that with these characters. I love everything about them. Their fire, their passion, their determination, and how they never give up.

Checkmate has probably been my favourite book to write so far. There is just something about their vibe and the whole story that consumed me from the moment that I started writing it, and I hope that you were as consumed by them as I was.

I want to say a big thank you to my alpha reader, cover designer and friend, Melanie A. Smith. She has once again been fantastic, and I can't believe that this is already the fifth book that she has designed the cover for. Melanie, you know I love you, so here's to many, many, many more alpha reads and delicious book covers, and thank you for all of your support, it means the world to me.

Of course, I couldn't have done this without the backing of two of my favourite ladies and beta readers, Nikki and Ashlee. These two have listened to my doubts, listened to my ideas, and they are there for me daily, making me smile and reminding me that I can absolutely do this. I love both of you ladies, and I am so thankful for our friendship.

To my ARC readers, thank you, thank you, thank you for signing up to read Checkmate. I hope you all enjoyed Paige and Joey's deliciously sinful ride.

I want to give a shout-out to the Badass Author Babes. You gals rock, thank you for making me laugh out loud in moments when I have needed it the most. Not only do you make me laugh, but you give the best advice and the support of our little crew is amazing.

And before I go, I have to tell you that, Checkmate is a stand-alone... BUT, those ideas that keep popping up in my head means that I am not quite ready to let these characters go yet...

I'll leave that thought there, but if you have already read my books, then you'll know that I am a massive fan of cliff-hangers, so it seems quite fitting to let you know that I am nowhere near done with these characters yet...

Until next time,
Much love,
Lindsey.

Made in the USA
Las Vegas, NV
29 April 2021